UNLEASHED BY HER BEAR

BLACK RIDGE BEARS BOOK 4

FELICITY HEATON

First printed September 2021

First Edition

Layout and design by Felicity Heaton

THE BLACK RIDGE BEARS SERIES

Book 1: Stolen by her Bear

Book 2: Rescued by her Bear

Book 3: Saved by her Bear

Book 4: Unleashed by her Bear

Book 5: Awakened by her Bear

The Black Ridge Bears series is part of the Eternal Mates World, which includes the Eternal Mates series, Cougar Creek Mates series, and the London Vampires series.

Discover more available paranormal romance books at:
http://www.felicityheaton.com

Or sign up to my mailing list to receive a FREE vampire romance ebook, learn about new titles, be eligible for special subscriber-only giveaways, and read exclusive content including short stories:
http://ml.felicityheaton.com/mailinglist

CHAPTER 1

Another wave of sickness rolled over her, bringing darkness in its wake again, and Callie fought it, fearing she would pass out. She couldn't pass out. She panted hard, each rapid breath stirring the old brown pine needles as she flopped onto her side, battling the encroaching darkness. She had to stay awake. If she passed out, she would shift, and if she shifted…

Sickness washed through her again, her stomach turning at just the thought.

So she waged a war against the pain that burned inside her, fire that seared her right hind leg and was growing stronger with every agonising second that trickled past. She waged a war with her body, refusing to let go of her wolf form, desperately clinging to it because the alternative didn't bear thinking about.

Callie mustered enough strength to continue her assault on the thick wire that had tightened around her right leg, twisted and frantically chewed on it. The metallic taste of it was joined with that of blood on her tongue as she bit closer to her leg. The snare had already cut deep into her flesh. If she couldn't get it loose, if she couldn't stop the pain from forcing her to shift back or the darkness from taking her, something that would also result in her returning to her human form, that snare was going to cause her a world of pain far worse than it was now.

As her ankle grew, the wire would slice into her flesh and hobble her by either causing a wound so deep she wouldn't be able to place weight on her leg or by snapping the bone. Hell, it might even take her foot clean off.

Wounds and broken bones she could mend, but she couldn't grow her foot back.

She snarled and growled, bit the wire and shook her head, trying to loosen it and free herself.

All the while aware of her surroundings, that at any moment the men who were after her could catch up with her.

She stilled, somehow made it through another wave of nausea that threatened to have her blacking out, and gave herself a moment to recover before attacking the old hunter's trap again. She couldn't afford to waste a second. She had to keep moving.

She had lost Carrigan and his men at the start of this valley, but every second she spent trying to free herself was a second that brought them closer to finding her.

She cursed and it came out as a mournful howl, something she regretted as the night went deathly still. That howl would carry for miles, giving away her position, but her wolf side was agitated, her instinct to call for help strong. Somewhere out there was White Wolf Lodge. She had to be close to it by now. If she called for help, someone might hear her and come to find her.

Someone might save her.

She should have reached that place of sanctuary by now, feared she had missed it somehow, even when she wasn't sure how that was possible. By all accounts, the lodge was large, with many tourist cabins on one side of the property, and just as many cabins for the wolf shifters who called it home on the other. It wasn't possible that she had managed to miss such a large group of cabins.

The urge to howl again rushed through her as the snare tightened further rather than loosening. Callie tamped it down, deeply aware that Carrigan was closing in on her, terrified of him finding her. Her heart laboured at just the thought, fear swift to sink sharp talons into her and seize hold of her, to shake and rattle her.

She couldn't go back to his pack.

She just couldn't.

The things he had threatened to do to her and the way the other males had looked at her, and the state of the females she had seen there, all ran around her head, tormenting her, working to tear down what little strength she had as they terrified her. She wasn't there now. She was free. Almost. She glared at the wire and started biting it again, shaking her head as she managed to get a fang into the loop, working it loose. She had escaped from that place, had narrowly avoided suffering the same terrible fate those females had, and she wasn't going back.

She wouldn't let him catch her.

She wouldn't.

If it came down to it, she would risk hobbling herself.

Gods, the thought of shifting back and allowing the wire to cut into her leg sickened her, hit her hard enough that she immediately changed her mind. She couldn't do it. She released the wire when her efforts to loosen it did nothing and flopped onto her side again, panting hard, needing a moment to breathe.

She had tried to shift back a few times, to let the snare slice into her ankle, but each time fear had stopped her.

Callie angled her head and stared through the canopy of the evergreen forest, past spindly pine and spruce branches and the thicker ones of the firs, gazing at the clear night sky. A million stars spotted it even in the smallest of gaps, the sight of them seeming to calm her as they gave her something else to focus on. A voice in the back of her mind whispered that she wasn't going to get out of this trap without shifting back, without accepting the pain that would come with her transformation into her human form. If she didn't find the strength to embrace that pain and do what was necessary, then Carrigan would find her.

Surely it was better to suffer a short burst of pain that would linger for a few days at most than subject herself to years of abuse? Years of being used by males who believed they owned her and had a right to her body. Years of living with males who looked down on her, treating her as inferior, as something that existed to serve them.

She huffed, blowing pine needles in all directions as her head dropped back to the ground.

All wolf packs were the same. Females were inferior, had few rights and never a say in anything, even in the more progressive packs in Canada. She had thought her pack different once, back when her family had been alive and she had been young and blind to the true nature of it. Then, when she had learned of the European packs and how many of them were making grand, sweeping changes to bring about equality, she had started to take a good hard look at her pack and hadn't liked what she had seen.

But even her pack had started looking progressive when she had seen the one Carrigan ran.

At least the males at her family's pack hadn't done as they pleased with females, taking them whether they were willing or not, slaking their urges whenever they struck with little regard for how it made the female feel.

Carrigan treated the female members of his pack as if they existed only to please the males.

Callie stared at the trunk of the nearest towering pine, the breeze stirring her black fur.

The White Wolf pack were meant to be different. More than just progressive. The alpha there believed in treating females with respect and kindness. He listened to them, even went as far as seeking their opinions about things and involving them in the running of his pack.

A pack that was made up of wolves from every corner of Canada and some from south of the border too.

According to the things she had heard, the pack alpha accepted anyone who came to him, no questions asked.

Gods, she hoped that was true.

She wouldn't blame him if he did turn her away though. She was bringing trouble in her wake, something he would have to deal with for her, and the closer she got to meeting him, the more she felt she was asking too much of a male she didn't know. She wasn't just asking him to take her in. She was asking him to fix her problem for her too.

Callie looked at her leg and the trap.

None of that mattered right now though. If she didn't escape this snare, she wouldn't even get the chance to find out whether the male would welcome her into his pack as he had everyone else. She would never know whether he might have dealt with her problem for her, or at the very least helped her deal with it.

Carrigan would find her and would drag her back to his pack.

She pulled herself together, shunning the part of her that wanted to give up, and sat up again. The wire was slick with her blood as she bit at it, getting her fang into the loop again, twisting her body at an awkward angle in order to make another attempt at loosening it.

Only she locked up tight as she heard a noise in the distance.

Her ears twitched, flicking back and forth, her senses reaching out in all directions as her heart laboured and fear mounted inside her. Was it Carrigan? One of his men?

The warm night breeze swirled around her, carrying the scent of pine needles and damp dirt.

And male.

But the rich, earthy scent wasn't one she recognised.

Callie looked at the wire looped around her right leg, dread pooling in her stomach. Was it the hunter come to claim his prize?

Panic seized her, fear that she was going to end up stuffed and mounted on display, or worse, her skin spread out as a rug before a fire, flooding her. She bolted into action on instinct, yelped as the wire pulled taut and cut into her flesh, reminding her she couldn't escape. Her instincts went haywire as fear rolled through her, bringing her primal ones to the fore. In her current form, it meant her wolf ones. The instinct to survive had her wrestling against the wire and no matter how hard she tried to shut it down, she couldn't calm herself enough to convince herself to stop trying to escape something that was inescapable.

The scent grew stronger, filling her lungs as she heard soft footsteps approaching her, and a strange calm came over her, eased her fear enough that she could think straight and wrest back control from her primal instincts. She didn't question it, just attacked the wire again, biting at it and shaking her head, loosening it.

And it was loosening.

Callie could almost taste her freedom.

A pair of heavy black boots stepped into view.

She locked up tight, fear drumming through her veins, her heart thundering as she slowly lifted her gaze.

Taking in the mountain of a male who was striding towards her with grim purpose.

Not a wolf.

Not a hunter either.

This towering brute who looked as if he was darkness made flesh in a black fleece that stretched tight over an impossibly broad chest and jeans that hugged legs like tree trunks, with his dark hair cut close to his scalp to reveal a deep scar that darted from his left temple to the crown of his head was something else.

And the look in his cold, emotionless pale blue eyes said he wanted to kill her.

CHAPTER 2

Rune seethed as he trekked through the darkness, swiftly navigating the dense forest that covered the sloping sides of the valleys. He didn't slow as he reached a practically sheer wall of dirt, kicked off and scaled it, his heightened vision allowing him to easily pick out roots and trees that clung to the steep cliff.

When he reached the top, he paused and tilted his head back, sniffed the air to catch the scent of the one who had dared to set foot in his pride's territory.

A wolf.

He growled through his fangs, blood on fire with a need to find the one who had howled, revealing their position close to Black Ridge. Anger churned his gut, had dark fur sweeping over his hands as he fought the urge to shift, as he battled the fierce hunger to fight.

A damned wolf.

His feet squelched in his wet boots as he stomped forwards, a bear on the warpath, determined to find the shifter and deal with them. His mood soured further as the damp lower half of his black jeans chilled and clung to his legs, irritating him with every step he took. He blamed the wolf for that too. He hadn't had time to remove his boots or roll up his jeans in order to cut through the creek that flowed through the heart of the clearing his pride called home.

A clearing that stood at the centre of their territory.

A territory this wolf shouldn't have set foot in.

When he found the one who had strayed into his territory, they were as good as dead.

None of their kind set foot on Black Ridge land and lived to tell the tale. He made sure of that.

Some dim, distant part of him screamed at him in a muffled voice that sounded as if it was far away or heard through layers of glass, telling him that he couldn't kill this wolf and he needed to rein in his dark desires.

His thoughts trod grim paths and he struggled to shift them to lighter ones as he stormed onwards, tracking the faint scent of fear and fur, his senses stretching around him, sharp enough that he could detect the heartbeats of even the smallest creatures in the forest. Those senses had been honed over the decades he had been a captive, locked onto anything that moved, just in case it meant to attack him. He had trained himself well, had taken great pains to make himself as sharp as a blade and as swift as the wind.

Had done whatever it had taken to survive.

He had never been a killer.

But gods, they had made him one.

Rune flexed his fingers and clenched his fists, paused to scent the air again as he picked up on a distant heartbeat.

The wolf?

Rather than launching in the direction he could feel the wretched beast waiting, he took a moment, drawing down great gulps of air to calm himself and steady his racing heart. There were no good wolves. In his opinion, none of them were to be trusted, all of them lacked a moral compass, and they were all out for themselves.

Saint believed differently though.

His alpha wanted the wolves who ventured too close or into Black Ridge territory to be driven out of it rather than slain. Saint had laid down that law after Rune had killed a wolf that had strayed onto the pride's property. In the years since then, Rune had managed to rein in his dark urges and had obeyed Saint and hadn't killed any more wolves.

But there had been a few close calls.

Sometimes, his past rolled up on him, stole control and made him react, that instinct to survive kicking in. It was him or them, and he always picked him.

He had a gut feeling that tonight was going to be one of those nights where he found it hard to resist killing. That darker part of himself was still snarling and growling, wanted him to deal with this wolf by spilling blood, and it was hard to rein it in and bring the quieter voice into focus, listening to it instead.

He had heard the howl when he had been at a celebration, surrounded by his pride and their latest addition. Knox and Skye were freshly mated, and the thought of a wolf being near her or any of the females that had recently joined their family had his mood running dark.

Dangerous.

The need to ensure Skye and Cameo, and even the little cougar female, Holly, were safe was strong, had overpowered him at times as he tracked the wolf, filling his mind with pleasing images of their broken carcass at his feet and their blood on his hands.

That same protective streak had seen him running along the creek for a good distance of his trek, using the water to cover his tracks and his scent, ensuring Maverick couldn't follow him. His friend meant well, only wanted to protect him too and make sure he was all right and handled things without losing his head, but Rune couldn't let him near the wolf.

The need to protect Maverick wasn't the only reason Rune had done everything in his power to lose him though. Deep in his heart he knew that Maverick would try to stop him from killing the wolf and Rune couldn't allow that.

Not this time.

If he killed the wolf, they couldn't hurt the females.

They couldn't hurt Maverick and his pride.

Wolves were cold. Manipulative. They were traitors.

All of them would hurt another in a heartbeat if it meant they gained something, and none of them cared about the welfare of others. They only cared about themselves.

Rune flexed his fingers again and growled through clenched fangs.

This wolf would be no different.

He had to kill it before it could hurt the females.

Rune ground to a halt and tightened his fists until his bones ached. No. He couldn't. He looked back in the direction of Black Ridge, not needing to be able to see through the dense canopy of the pines, spruces and firs to see it. He could see it in his mind. Could always see it.

Home.

The only home he had ever really known.

Or at least could remember.

He couldn't kill the wolf. He felt that in his soul, deep beyond the part of him that raged with a need to spill blood, to protect the females at any cost. To protect his pride.

He wouldn't have a pride if he slaughtered the beast as he wanted.

Saint would be furious with him, and gods, he didn't want that. That deeply buried part of him was still waiting for the male to wise up and kick him out of his pride, to realise that allowing him to join it all those decades ago, together with Maverick, had been a mistake.

Rune drew another slow, deep breath, calming his raging need to lash out at the wolf and kill it. Satisfied that he would be able to control himself, he trekked onwards, picking up the trail again. It led him towards one of the mountains, and he frowned and paused again as he found an animal track. There were hundreds of them that crossed through the forest, trails made by years of every beast that lived in the valley using them, whether that was ungulates like the white-tailed deer and moose, or predators like the cougars and bears.

This one was a popular route along one side of the valley, following the line of the mountains, and it led towards somewhere.

An old hunter's cabin.

It was a long way from Black Ridge, just outside the pride's territory. The thought that the wolf might be heading towards it gave him comfort, easing his fears, but also had his thoughts darkening again.

If he killed the wolf out there, by that cabin, Saint would never know.

He could lie to his alpha and tell him that the wolf had run.

Rune clenched his fists again. No. He wouldn't lie to Saint. He would never lie to him. Saint had been good to him, had given him more than just shelter and food. He had given Rune a home. A pride.

And he took great pains to make sure that both Rune and Maverick had everything they needed, were both on their way to leading normal lives again.

So he would never lie to Saint.

He would drive the wolf away and that would be that.

His need to get rid of the wolf before it could cause hurt to the pride would be sated and he could return to the celebration before Maverick or Saint worried about him. Gods, Maverick was going to be worried sick about him. For a tough bear, Maverick had a good heart. He just couldn't see it. Right now, having lost Rune's trail, that heart would be filled with fear, with thoughts as dark as Rune's had been over the last few miles.

Rune was going to have to apologise to him when he returned to the Ridge.

And maybe take a few punches.

Maverick had a bad tendency to do his talking with his fists.

Rune eased to a crouch beside the trail and touched the various paw prints that had been left in the dirt, experience allowing him to pick out even the barest trace of a mark. The scuff of claws was enough to tell him which breed of animal had used the track in the last day, and he easily picked out the tell-tale sign of a wolf shifter.

The grooves dug into the dirt by claws were unmistakably wolf, but the print was too large to be that of the animal variety. Wolf shifters were larger than their animal counterparts. The difference was only the matter of around one hundred pounds, but it was noticeable.

Rune teased some of the dirt in the print loose, brought it to his nose and sniffed it. Definitely wolf. Definitely shifter. The scent had a manufactured note to it, one that reeked of perfume or cologne. One that riled him for some reason, had his mood taking a sharp dark turn and his fangs dropping.

He stood and followed the tracks, picking up pace again as his focus locked onto the distinct shape and size of the paw prints. Everything else fell away, nothing else mattering to him in that moment. He didn't care about the cougar prints that crossed the path or the distant grunt of a moose. Didn't care as smaller nocturnal creatures skittered about the forest floor in search of food or the birds in the trees watched him as he passed.

He only cared about the wolf.

About finding it and driving it away.

Or killing it.

Gods, he wanted to kill the owner of that scent. He wanted to rip them apart with his bare hands. He wanted to make them pay for crossing into his territory, for daring to come near his pride.

He tamped down that need, wrestled with himself and somehow found the strength to deny the need to kill.

A rapid heartbeat reached his ears and he slowed to a jog and then a walk, his senses reaching out into the forest around him and instantly narrowing as soon as he detected the owner of that trembling heart.

That fearful heart.

Rune eased through the darkness like a shadow, slowly closing the distance between him and the wolf, his eyebrows knitting hard as he focused on it. It was in distress. Why? Because it knew he was coming?

The scent of fear hung heavily in the air, but couldn't quite mask the other smell he detected as he closed in on the wolf.

Blood.

Rune steadied himself, breathing deeply to get oxygen into his muscles, to prepare his body for a potential fight to the death—a fight he would win.

As soon as he felt ready, he shifted a step to his right, emerging from behind the thick trunk of a lodgepole pine.

Only he wasn't prepared for the sleek black wolf he spotted just feet in front of him.

A female.

She desperately tried to bite at something, twisting around towards her hind leg, and snarled as she wrestled with it.

Rune wanted to snarl too when he shifted his focus there and saw why she was scared and why he smelled blood. The wire of a snare wrapped tightly around her right leg and cut into her dark fur. A hunter's trap.

He stepped out of the shadows.

She froze, amber eyes lifting to him.

She panted hard as she stared across the narrow span of forest floor to him.

Rune caught the pain in her eyes, and the fear too. He looked at the snare that held her at his mercy, bared his fangs at the evil device as it hit him that she knew she couldn't shift back into her human form and she was desperately holding on to her animal one.

If she shifted, the wire would cut into her ankle as it thickened. At the very least, it would slice deeply into her flesh. If she wasn't as lucky, it would break the bone.

Rune met her gaze again.

Determined one thing about her, something that resonated with him.

She was a fighter.

She had to be, because usually pain caused their kind to shift back into their human forms. The fact she was still in her wolf form revealed the depth of her fortitude and how desperate she was not to hurt herself.

He stared at her in silence, debating whether to finish her off, but as she continued to gaze up at him, he found he couldn't bring himself to do it. He had a chance to kill a wolf, and he couldn't.

She was waiting for it. He could see it in her eyes. She was waiting for death and for some unnerving reason, he didn't like it.

In fact, he hated it.

Rune shoved aside all his feelings, purging them and allowing a cold and calculating sort of calm to wash through him instead. The same calm he had used countless times to focus his mind and his body before a fight.

Only this battle wasn't going to be fought with fist and fang. It was going to be fought with words. Something he wasn't accustomed to doing, but he would learn on the fly because he wanted to know what a lone wolf female was doing up in the valley.

Of course, that meant he needed her to shift back so she could answer his questions.

He doubted she was going to come quietly. That edge her amber eyes were slowly gaining said he might have to fight her after all. Dangerous. If they fought, he might not be able to control himself. He might not be able to stop himself from hurting her.

And for some damned reason, he didn't want to hurt her.

Rune mentally prepared himself, steeled his mind and told himself that he could take a few hits if it meant she survived to answer his questions. He could.

She snarled and bared fangs at him as he approached her, even though he held his palms out in front of him, trying to show her that tonight was her lucky night and he wasn't going to kill her. When he eased into a squat near her rear quarters, she snapped at him and tried to move, yelped as the wire pulled taut and cut deeper into her flesh.

"Idiot," he muttered and grabbed the wire, intending to pull it towards him to loosen the grip it had on her.

She really didn't like that.

In a lightning-fast move, she whipped around and sank her fangs into his left forearm, growling the whole time.

Rune flinched and growled right back at her as pain burned up his arm, as warm blood slid over his skin beneath his black fleece, but he didn't miss a beat. By lunging for him, she had moved closer to him, loosening the wire. He let her use his arm as a chew toy as he tugged at the loop of the wire with his other hand.

The second the loop was large enough for her to free her leg, she released his arm and made a break for it.

Rune grabbed her by her scruff, fisting it hard, and pinned her to the ground. She snarled, wriggled and desperately tried to break free, her good rear leg scrabbling around in the pine-needle-strewn dirt, stirring the scent into the cooling night air.

"Not so fast, little wolf. I've got questions and you're going to answer them."

He growled and shoved her down. Her amber gaze slid to lock with his. His mood took a sharp, dark turn as anger shone in her eyes, as he realised that she wasn't going to give him what he wanted, and the bite marks she had left on his arm throbbed and stung. He let his claws out and dug them into her skin, giving himself a better grip on her and making it clear she wasn't going anywhere.

"You're going to answer my questions."

Rune held her gaze.

Snarled.

"If you don't, you won't live to taste that freedom I just gave you."

CHAPTER 3

Callie had gone from one bad situation to another. She growled as the big male manhandled her, tightly gripping her scruff, his nails piercing her skin, making it sting. Payback. It was payback for what she had done to him. He wanted to hurt her, to make her bleed as she had him, and wanted her to know that out of the two of them, he was the stronger and more dangerous.

Anger and fear were joined by irritation and a serious dose of shame as he stood in one fluid motion and hauled her into the air with him. He held her aloft before him, as if she weighed nothing, the muscles of his right arm flexing hard beneath his form-fitting black zip-up fleece. Fire blazed in her scruff where he held her in a vice-like grip, her weight pulling on it as she hung from his hand, her legs dangling above the dirt.

Callie reacted fiercely, the feeling he was mocking her rousing a reaction in her that she couldn't contain. She couldn't stop herself from twisting and snarling, snapping her fangs at him and shaking her head. The bastard was belittling her. He was making it painfully clear that she was no match for him. That feeling grew, spread poisoned tendrils through her mind as he just stared at her, his pale blue eyes ice-cold and impassive. She kicked her back legs, jerking her entire body in a bid for freedom.

He only tightened his grip in response.

She bared fangs at him, kept on growling and snarling, viciously snapping her teeth at him. He was right to hold on to her. If he released her, she would sink her fangs into somewhere that would be far more painful for him than his arm.

The big brute arched a dark eyebrow at her.

As if her fury, this rage that burned inside her, born of the fact he was drawing a line between them by holding her like this, by easily caging her, meant nothing to him. She wasn't weak. She might be female, but she was strong, and if he let her go, she would prove that. She would make him see that he was wrong about her, and about females in general. She would rewrite his opinion of her gender in blood.

His blood.

"Calm down," he grunted as she made another attempt to wriggle free of his grip.

Easy for him to say. He wasn't the one being held at someone else's mercy, threatened with death if he didn't answer their questions.

The wolf in her said to keep struggling, keep fighting, and she would escape his hold. The more logical side of her brain said that there was only one way out of this. She wasn't sure she wanted to take it.

She settled and slowly swung towards him as she went still, allowing her to see him. To see those cold eyes. That scar that said he was a fighter. The hard and unyielding cut of his mouth as his lips flattened.

Callie had never been shy, but something about this male made her acutely aware of how naked she would be if she shifted back.

It was the only way to make him release her though.

At least, she hoped he would release her.

The alternative didn't bear thinking about.

"Wolves," he scoffed, spitting that word as if it was disgusting to him. He sneered, his lip curling, and muttered, "Should've known you'd have a bent moral compass too. You're all the same. Thinking you can do as you please. Thinking only of yourselves."

The look in his eyes shifted, backing up his words and making her feel he would rather kill her than spend another second in her company.

It was the last straw.

Callie willed the shift, giving up her fight to hold on to her wolf form. Her feet easily touched the ground as her body morphed, bones lengthening and changing as her fur swept away to reveal flushed skin.

Skin that flushed even deeper pink as she grew intensely aware of his gaze on her naked curves.

She turned to face him, covering her awkwardness by stoking her anger, denying the hot flash of desire that rolled through her by focusing on her rage, on the fury born of what he had said to her, speaking of her as if she was despicable.

He didn't know her.

She planted her hands on her hips and glared at him. "What's your problem?"

The brute stared right back at her and growled, "You're my problem."

Callie swept her left arm up and knocked his hand away from her nape, must have caught him off guard because he looked pissed as he lost his grip on her. He lunged for her and she hopped back a step, placing herself beyond his reach and making sure she landed on her good leg.

She flicked her fall of black hair over her shoulder and tipped her chin up, and tersely said, "Thanks for freeing me. I'll be on my way now. No more problem for you."

She went to turn.

He seized her wrist.

Callie smacked his hand away again, growled at him and bared her fangs. "Keep your filthy paws to yourself, buddy."

His pale blue eyes flashed with chilling fire, with rage she knew she was stoking, but she couldn't bring herself to heel. Something about him riled her, rubbed her the wrong way, made her want to push and fight him despite his size and how strong he was.

Maybe she was just sick and tired of overbearing males thinking they could order her around.

He proved how overbearing he was by saying, "Answer my questions and I'll think about letting you go."

She huffed at that. "How kind of you. I'll skip the answering questions part and move straight to the leaving, thanks."

He made another grab for her.

Callie was on to him, moved too quickly for him to keep up, nimbly leaping away from him to place a good ten feet of dirt between them. She grimaced when she placed some weight on her right leg as she landed and pain shot up it, arcing along her bones.

He growled, only this time it was a low groaning sound that bordered on sorrowful or oddly melancholy, and it sent a shiver down her spine and rang alarm bells in her head as it revealed what he was.

A bear.

She had never had a good experience with a bear shifter. They were ridiculously territorial, almost as bad as the felines. Felines were worse though. She wanted to spit on the ground at just the thought of them, while at the same time she wanted to run as fast as her tired, aching legs could carry her.

The term 'fighting like cats and dogs' was applicable in the shifter world too. Callie had lost count of the number of fights she had gotten into with a feline shifter just because she was a wolf.

"If you won't answer me, then you'll answer to my alpha." Bear was surprisingly quick, closed the distance between them without giving himself away, and had his hand on her arm before she could blink and catch up.

She had been watching him closely, should have spotted the moment he decided to move. He hadn't broadcasted his intent at all though. One moment he had been standing there, as calm as anything and showing no sign he was going to try something, and the next he was right beside her.

For some reason, that terrified her.

Who was this male? Or better still, what was he? She had never seen a male move like he did. Not even the warriors at her old pack had moved like him, without broadcasting anything to the enemy. When she had watched them sparring, something she had often done because she wasn't allowed to fight since she was female, she had always been able to spot when they would move. The slightest shift of their weight. The smallest change in their eyes. Even a secretly drawn breath. There had always been a tell, something to warn her they would make a move against their sparring partner, something most of the warriors always seemed to fail to notice.

But not her.

She had been good at spotting them.

Which was why she knew he hadn't given away his intent to move.

She stared up into his eyes as he loomed over her, easily a good nine inches taller than her despite the fact she was pushing five-eleven, was tall for a wolf female. A cold abyss stared back at her. No trace of emotion. Not even rage.

Everything about him was carefully, meticulously controlled.

Right down to his breathing and the pressure of his grip on her arm. Not hard enough to hurt her, or gentle enough that she could twist free. He held her just tightly enough that she knew she couldn't escape him, not without resorting to a desperate act of violence. Even then, she had her doubts it would be enough to break free of his grip this time.

Callie studied him, swiftly cataloguing everything about this dark male, this dangerous bear.

Was he a warrior too?

If he was, he was on another level to those she had known back at her old pack, back when her life had been better.

It struck her that Bear hadn't moved in the whole time she had been staring at him, had locked up tight, as if placing his filthy paw on her had startled him. If it had, nothing about him other than his stillness gave it away.

Callie found herself relaxing a little, some of the tension draining from her when he made no move to hurt her or drag her somewhere, just stood there watching her, his eyes glacial. She wanted to break through that layer of ice for some reason, felt compelled to provoke him and gain a reaction. Some twisted part of her wanted to crack the cage around his emotions wide open and see what came out.

She raked her eyes over him, an appraising look that she hoped rankled him. "You're not the alpha?"

He was a big male. Bigger than any wolf she had ever met. He had to be twice Carrigan's size. Outmuscled even Carrigan's biggest goon.

If Bear was this big, then how big was his leader?

She didn't want to find out.

"I'm good." Those words came out as flippant as she meant them to, had a flicker of cold fire igniting in his eyes again. "I don't need to meet your extended family. I'll just be on my way."

"On your way where?" He tightened his grip on her arm, the barest flex of his fingers. It was enough to deliver the silent message that she wasn't going anywhere.

Not until she answered his questions.

Well, they were both shit out of luck then. She wasn't going to tell him anything about herself, because it was safer that way, and he wasn't going to let her go. A stalemate. She looked at him, her resolve wavering. He was from this valley, lived here and must have come to find her when she had howled, dispatched by his pack to locate her and bring her in for questioning.

Which meant he would probably be able to tell her whether or not the White Wolf pack was near here.

She needed to reach that pack and soon. Every second she spent here with Bear was another second that Carrigan closed in on her.

The longer she stared into his eyes, locked in a stalemate with him, the stronger a feeling grew inside her—Bear wouldn't answer her questions. He wanted to ask his and hear her answer them, and that was that. She had met males like him in the past, ones who were rigid about how they went about things, inflexible and unlikely to bend to accommodate others.

Her eyes widened as he tried to prove her wrong about him, as he released her arm and eased back a step, placing some distance between them. Maybe he wasn't as bad as she was painting him.

She thought he might be worse when he unzipped his thick fleece and pulled it off, stripping down to only a black T-shirt that hugged his heavily-muscled torso like a second skin.

"What are you doing?" She hated that note of panic in her voice, how her words warbled and how he looked at her as if she was weak.

Or perhaps insane to fear he wanted to do anything nefarious to her.

"I'm tired of seeing you naked." He held the fleece out to her. "Put it on."

"No." Callie stood her ground, ignoring the way her cheeks heated as he stared at her, as a voice in the back of her mind taunted her for fearing he had been about to try something with her when she apparently wasn't attractive enough for him.

Her blood burned for another reason as that hit her. Plenty of males had told her she was beautiful and had pursued her, desiring her as their lover. Some of them had wanted her to be more than that for them, and while she had been flattered, she had turned them all down. None of them had been quite right for her.

They hadn't ignited the spark she wanted to feel, the one that came from finding a true mate. She wanted a love like her parents had shared—the love only capable between fated mates.

Callie told herself that she would find that love one day.

What did it matter that Bear wasn't attracted to her? What did it matter that, judging by the look in his eyes, he found her repulsive? That was a good thing. It meant he was unlikely to try anything with her. It meant she was safe.

"Put it on, Wolf." He shoved the fleece towards her again, his rough features hardening like granite. "I'm taking you to Black Ridge. You're going to answer to my alpha and if you want to do that naked, it's up to you… but there are unmated males at the pride."

She tensed.

Unmated males that Bear clearly felt would ogle her and want to do things to her if she was nude. She wasn't attractive enough for Bear, but he believed she would be alluring enough to these males.

She didn't want him to feel he had scored a victory over her, but she snatched the fleece and pulled it on, was quick to zip it up. She paused with her hand near her throat as his scent hit her—rich, earthy, warm. Her eyes lifted and locked with his, her fingers lingering on the tab of the zipper, her thoughts twisting and twining together. She felt unsteady as she gazed into his eyes, as something crossed them, a flicker of feelings that were there and gone in a heartbeat, erased before she could decipher them.

She convinced herself to release the zipper and tried not to think about how she was wearing something of his and how it carried his scent—scent that was now stamped all over her. There was something pleasing about the way he smelled, something that eased her tension and her fear. No. It wasn't his scent doing that. She told herself that on repeat. It was the fact she was covered now, the warm fleece concealing everything from her shoulders to midway down her thighs. She was covered and that was the reason she felt safer.

It had nothing to do with Bear's scent.

She thought about what he had said about the bears at this Black Ridge place where he wanted to take her.

Did Bear have a mate? He didn't strike her as the sort of male who had one. He had too many rough edges for that, but stranger things had happened.

Someone in this world might have thought the brute act appealing.

Bear continued to look at her, his gaze searing her despite the fact it was devoid of emotions, the thick impenetrable layer of ice concealing what he was thinking. She wanted to know what was running through his mind, couldn't hold her tongue as he remained standing close to her rather than distancing himself as she had expected.

She angled her head back, tipping it up towards his, and whispered.

"Why are you staring at me?"

CHAPTER 4

Rune wasn't about to answer that question and he certainly wasn't going to examine the way he had reacted to the female over the last few minutes. She had surprised him by shifting back while still in his grasp, enough that she had easily escaped his hold, and then she had stood there as bold as brass, naked and full of spit and fire.

He hadn't quite known where to look, but his eyes had decided that searing the image of her on his memory was a good place to start.

Which had unnerved him enough that he had made what he now felt was a monumental mistake.

He had tried to cover her up and in his infinite wisdom, he had offered his fleece, and now she was wearing it, her sinful curves draped in the black material his body had warmed, his scent stamped all over her, obliterating that trace of perfume he had smelled on her.

It was enough to throw him for a loop, had him standing as still as a statue and staring at her, lost in the conflict that raged within him, swept up in it to the point where if she wanted to run, he probably wouldn't be able to snap himself out of his thoughts to stop her.

She eyed him closely, a shrewd edge to her large amber eyes, and he wanted to bare his teeth at her and warn her to stop staring at him. Ironic, he knew. He couldn't stop staring at her, but her staring at him made him angry, made him want to lash out at her and drive her away.

Or maybe it was how she made him feel that had him reacting violently to her presence.

He didn't like the way she affected him, how unsteady she made him, how she left him feeling unsure of what to do or how to handle her. He wanted answers from her, had threatened to turn her over to Saint, but the more he thought about taking her to Black Ridge, the more he wanted to walk her in the opposite direction to his pride's home.

Because he needed to protect them from a possible threat.

That was the only reason he didn't want to take her to the Ridge.

It had nothing to do with the thought of her being near Maverick. *Maverick.* Was his friend still out there searching for his trail or had sense kicked in to tell him to return to the Ridge to wait for him? Rune hoped it was the latter.

He looked at the wolf, knew he should take her to the Ridge to ease his friend's mind by returning to his side, and also show Saint that he had resisted the urge to kill another wolf. He couldn't though.

Rune came up with a multitude of reasons why he shouldn't take her to Black Ridge straight away.

He could get her to answer his questions and might be able to release her without ever needing to reveal where his pride lived. It was dark and her injury would make it difficult to get her through the forest without incident, and he was damned if he was going to carry her. There was a place nearby where he could easily spend the night with the wolf and carry out his business, without having to involve Saint, proving that he could handle things by himself without surrendering to his need to kill all wolves.

Rune seized her arm as resolve flowed through him and tugged her towards the hunter's cabin that was barely a few hundred feet from him, closer to the mountain.

"Where are you taking me?" She twisted her wrist in his grip, her words coming out clipped and harsh, full of the anger he could sense in her. "Let me go. I'm not going to meet your alpha."

"You're right about that." He yanked her forwards, refusing to feel bad when her injured ankle gave out and she hit the dirt on her knees, tugging him backwards as he kept hold of her arm.

Rune pulled her back onto her feet. She glared at him rather than thanked him.

"Son of a bitch," she snarled, baring short fangs, and turned her wrist again, didn't seem to care that she was hurting herself. "Let me go."

She battered his arm with her other hand.

When she lunged her head towards him, clearly intending to sink fangs into him again, he jerked her arm up, throwing her aim off. He lifted his hand higher and she grunted and rose onto her tiptoes, desperately trying to remain in contact with the ground.

"You keep on fighting me and we're going to fall out." He bared his teeth as he squared up to her.

She pulled a face and tried to use her weight against him, her muscles flexing as she bounced in his grip, attempting to pull his arm down. He tightened his grip on her wrist, showing her that it wasn't going to work.

She surprised him by lifting her bare feet and pressing them to his thigh. She leaned backwards, her jaw clenching as she heaved, as she shoved against his leg while pulling on his arm.

Getting nowhere.

"Wolf," he growled in warning, haemorrhaging patience as she made another pathetic attempt to escape his hold.

Her eyes shone bright amber.

His narrowed on her as awareness swept through him. "You even think about shifting and I'll shift too. You're injured and I know this terrain better than you. You honestly think you can outrun me?"

He grabbed her other arm when she threw a punch at him.

Yanked her against him and caged her with his arm around her back, pinning her to his chest.

"Think hard, Wolf. You want six-hundred pounds of angry bear bearing down on you?"

Her panted breaths washed over his face, bathing his skin with their warmth, making him hyper-aware of how close she was to him, how he had pulled her against him, pressing her body to his. He really hadn't thought it through. By pulling her to him, he had made her feet slip from his thigh.

A thigh she now straddled, the apex of her legs pressed against it, her heat seeping into him.

Gods.

Fear lit her eyes, the sight of it enough to have him shoving her away from him and averting his gaze. He kept hold of her wrist, but loosened his grip, couldn't bring himself to look at her as she tugged the hem of the fleece she wore down, her hand unsteady.

Shaking as badly as he was inside.

He cursed himself, cursed her too for good measure, and pulled her with him, leading her to the cabin. She followed him in silence, not helping matters. Where was her spit and fire now when he needed her to be loud and rude, to fill this tense silence with noise?

To show him that he hadn't just crossed a line with her.

"Why can't you just let me go?" she murmured and he resisted the temptation to look back at her, knew that if he did the softer part of him that had somehow survived his years in captivity would make him want to do just that.

It didn't come to the fore often, but when it did, he ended up looking like some weak, pathetic sap.

A bear with a big heart.

Rune crushed that part of him and shoved it back down deep, where the wolf wouldn't see it. He didn't remember the male he had been before the arena, before Archangel hunters had shaped him into the beast he was today, but sometimes he had the feeling he had been soft, warm of heart, perhaps even gentle.

He wasn't that male anymore though.

"I told you. I want you to answer some questions. You're the one making this more difficult than it needs to be." He led her around a tree, his gaze scanning the darkness ahead of them as his senses reached out in all directions, trying to pinpoint the cabin. "Just answer the questions, Wolf, and then maybe you can be on your way."

"Maybe?" she bit out.

And there was that spark he was coming to admire in her, the spit and fire that she used as a shield to protect herself. For a female, she had strength. Not just physically. She was strong mentally too. Many females would have broken down if they had been in her position, succumbing to fear.

Not this wolf.

She had spirit.

Courage.

Either someone had raised her to be strong, or life had moulded her into a warrior.

Rune wanted to ask her which it was, but held his tongue. He had no reason to ask her such a thing. No desire to learn more about her personal life. He needed to stick to the important questions, ones that her answers to would determine whether he let her go or not. He wasn't here to be her friend.

Wasn't interested in being more than that either.

She started battering his hand again. "Maybe isn't good enough, buddy. Let me go. You have no right to hold me like this."

Rune turned on her, flashing fangs as he growled, "I have every right. You trespassed into Black Ridge territory."

She locked up tight, a flicker of fear in her eyes that was gone in an instant as she reared her head forwards and cracked it against his. He grunted as pain shot outwards from the point of impact, snarled and seized her by her throat when his sharp senses warned she was going to headbutt him again. He gritted his teeth as he closed his fingers around her throat, fighting the urge to squeeze, to repay her for hurting him.

He scoffed at that.

Hurting him?

Irritating him then. Her blow had been weak, not nearly enough to fell him. The fiends who had held him captive had moulded him into a killer, had told him time and again that he had a hard head. He could take a blow from a male ten times her size and strength and not black out.

Her amber eyes edged downwards, towards the hand he had locked around her throat.

"I'm being nice here, Wolf. You want to find out what happens when I'm not nice?" He squared up to her and growled down into her face, refusing to let her sharp intake of breath affect him. "I got real good reasons not to trust any of your breed. So if you want to keep pushing me… keep on pushing. You won't like what happens when I push back."

She stared at him in silence.

He held her gaze, looking deep into her eyes, into amber cast with bright golden sparks of fire and tiny flecks of darkness. There was a fighter locked behind those eyes, a female who wanted to lash out at him and keep on pushing him, provoking his darker side. Why? What had happened to this female to make her want to take on the world? To make her so angry at it and everyone in it?

Sure, he deserved her wrath for how he was treating her and the fact he was holding her, but his gut said that rage and hurt he could read in her eyes, feelings that made it hard for her to control her reactions around him, had nothing to do with him. Not really.

Someone had hurt this female.

Deeply.

Rune loosened his grip on her throat, easing his fingers open, but couldn't convince himself to break contact with her. Her throat worked on a hard swallow, her pulse fluttering against his fingers as she stared up at him. Not just her pulse. Her entire body was shaking as she stood before him, as a war erupted in her eyes, one that had them edging away from him, towards a point over her right shoulder.

Towards the place where the mountains that enclosed the valley met the highway.

Rune looked there too. "Why are you running?"

She whipped to face him, surprise shining in her eyes. Shocked that he could read her well enough to know she was running from something?

And she was running scared.

His mood took another dark turn.

"Is it hunters?" he growled, the urge to forget her and rush back to the Ridge flooding him. "Is it Archangel?"

The mortal hunter organisation were monsters, thrived on hunting and harming his kind and hers. Their façade of a peaceful group who only targeted dangerous non-humans fooled many in their world, but he knew the other side of that mask. He had seen just how twisted and cruel, how evil, that organisation truly was.

She was quick to shake her head. "No."

An answer at last. It seemed the little wolf didn't want to meet Death tonight, didn't want him associating her with Archangel and convincing himself that she was working with them or had led them to this valley.

To his home.

"Someone is after you, and I want to know who it is." He turned away from her and tugged her towards the cabin.

It was close now. He took determined strides towards it, the need to reach shelter driving him forwards. Just in case Wolf was lying like all her breed had a tendency to do.

The cabin would provide cover, allowing him to keep an eye on his surroundings without exposing himself, and giving him time to question the female and get the answers he wanted.

Rune glared over his shoulder at her.

Answers he would get one way or the other.

CHAPTER 5

Callie revised her previous thought as Bear dragged her through the woods, looking ready to murder her and bury her body where no one would find it. She hadn't gone from one bad situation to another.

She had gone from being in shit to being in deep shit. Up to her neck level deep shit.

She tossed a glance at her surroundings, gaze darting everywhere as she hobbled along behind the big brute, seeking an escape route even when she knew he was right. Running would get her nowhere. She could probably manage a shift, but her leg was in agony, would slow her down or force her back out of her wolf form. She was too tired now, wasn't sure she would be able to hold on to her other form if she shifted and the pain became too much.

Bear would easily catch her and she was starting to believe that his threats weren't idle ones. He wasn't trying to scare her. He was just speaking the truth. If she ran, he would catch her, and she would end up on the receiving end of the barely-leashed anger that had flashed in his eyes a moment ago.

When he had thought she was running from Archangel.

She had no love for the hunter organisation herself, but the spark of cold fire that had lit his eyes had made it clear that he despised Archangel and everyone in it, giving her the impression he'd had some bad personal experiences with them.

Really bad.

In her life, she had met a few people who had suffered at the hands of Archangel, whether it was through the hunters murdering family members during a raid or because they had taken them captive for a time.

None of them had looked fit to kill someone just because they thought they might be leading hunters from that organisation towards their home.

She wasn't sure Bear believed her when she said she wasn't involved with them, and she wasn't sure he would believe a word she said if she did tell him why she was running. She wasn't really sure of anything where this male was concerned. Something about him had her off-balance, had her acting out of character. She had been raised a good wolf, an obedient female despite her desire to break the invisible chains that bound her, keeping her in her place.

Something about Bear made her wild, feral, made it impossible to control herself. Headbutting him had been a terrible idea, and she had known it, but some part of her, some instinct deep within her, had pushed her to do it.

Had pushed her to push him.

She had never had a death wish before, but she felt certain this was what one felt like.

She meant to be calm and controlled around Bear, meant to do as he wanted and not incite him.

Only she kept ending up doing the opposite.

She huffed when all she saw were trees, trees and more trees. The night was a deep dark without a moon to brighten it, made it hard for her to make out anything beyond thirty or forty feet. If she ran, she could end up running straight off an earth cliff like the one she had been forced to scale before she had been caught in the trap. The last thing she needed was to hurt herself even worse than she already was.

What she really needed to do was heal, but that meant she needed time to rest, and that meant Carrigan would be closing the distance between them. Unless how dark it was tonight without the moon forced him to rest too. Trying to track her in the darkness would be difficult, even if he had her scent to follow. For all his faults, Carrigan was a shrewd male, one who might decide it was more sensible for him and his men to rest for the night to recover their strength and then pursue her at daybreak.

Which meant she might have until dawn before she had to make another run for it.

She glanced at the back of Bear's head, at a small number and letter tattooed on his spine just above the collar of his black T-shirt.

082-B.

"Odd tattoo." Her voice sounded loud in the darkness.

Bear's shoulders stiffened and he tossed a black look at her before he faced front again.

And tugged on his T-shirt so the collar rose up enough to cover the tiny inked number and letter.

What did it mean? Did B stand for Bear?

She frowned as a possible explanation hit her. Was her theory that Bear had a bad history with Archangel right, and for some reason the hunter group had tattooed him with this number? She had never heard of Archangel marking non-humans in such a way, but maybe they did.

It would explain why he seemed so ashamed of it and hadn't wanted her to see it.

She wanted to ask about it, that part of her that, for some godsdamned reason, wanted to provoke Bear mingling with the part of her that was curious about him. Only a cabin emerged from the gloom ahead of her, capturing her attention. Her pulse drummed faster, fear swift to shoot into her veins as she stared at the old, run-down log cabin and then at the back of Bear's head.

Callie leaned back and tugged on his arm, trying to break free of his hold as fear got the better of her again, filled her mind with images she tried to shut out. Bear looked back at her, his dark eyebrows knitting hard above icy eyes.

Icy eyes that softened a little as they met hers. A mirage. She was imagining that slight thawing, that almost regretful edge they gained before they hardened again and he turned away from her.

"Not going to hurt you, Wolf." His bass voice rolled over her, smooth and even, no trace of malevolence in it. "Just need to find us some shelter for the night. You can rest that leg while you answer my questions."

The effect his words had on her was instantaneous. The fear that had blasted through her fell away, the images her tired mind was throwing at her swift to dissipate, and she relaxed a little as she hobbled along behind him. For all his glowering at her, his threats and his gruffness, Bear was a gentleman.

More so than the wolves in Carrigan's pack anyway.

Gods, she hated how her short time there had coloured her opinion of all males, had made her expect every one of them to be like them—thinking they could just have any female they wanted, whether she wanted it or not.

She sighed.

Bear angled his head slightly towards her and then faced forwards. He took the steps up onto the rickety deck of the small cabin and opened the door while she mounted them behind him. She gripped the frame of the door as she followed him into the room, her hand trailing off it as she took in her surroundings and limped forwards.

Her eyes struggled to adjust to the darkness, but she could make out a few things. Like the fact this cabin was tiny—one small room. No one had lived here in a long time either. There wasn't even a kitchen. A few poorly constructed cabinets lined the wall to her right and there was a bench beneath the window near the door. The drapes were tattered and didn't fully cover the window as Bear pulled them closed with one hand.

The fingers of his other hand slowly flexed around her wrist. For a cold bastard, he had warm hands. He helped her forwards, deeper into the room, and turned her and eased her down into a wooden chair. It creaked beneath her. Probably had woodworm or was so ancient it was going to turn to dust at any moment.

Bear released her, went to the door and closed it. He rifled through the cupboards. Looking for food? She didn't even want to think about what he might find to eat in a place like this. She pulled a face at it as she took it in. Besides the log burner to her right, that had to be one of the first ever made, there was a small worn bed behind her that looked ready to collapse, and two more wooden chairs, both to her left.

Maybe she could help Bear out by getting a fire going. She didn't want to alert Carrigan to her location, but she also didn't want to freeze to death.

She went to move and Bear shot to his feet and pivoted to face her.

"Sit," he growled and she glared at him.

Or more specifically, what he was holding in his right hand.

"Here I thought you were being civilised and nice by helping me to this chair." Callie kept her eyes locked on the rope that dangled from his fingers. The urge to bolt was strong, but she kept her ass planted to the chair, aware that the only way out of the cabin was near Bear. "Is that really necessary?"

"I don't trust you," he gritted.

"I get the feeling you don't trust anyone," she countered and swallowed as he closed the distance between them in only two strides, came to tower over her, looming like a shadow in the darkness.

At least outside, the faint light of the stars had been enough to reveal his features to her, giving her a chance at knowing what he was thinking. As she stared up into the inky gloom at his face, her eyes adjusted to reveal it to her, but not as clearly as she had been able to see him outside. What she could make out about him didn't help at all.

His rough features were a stony mask, his eyes revealing nothing to her.

He eased around behind her, grabbed her arms and tugged them back. Callie yanked her right one free, was tempted to elbow him in the groin, but stopped herself at the last second. Angering Bear wasn't going to get her anywhere. Well, it wouldn't get her anywhere other than dead.

He grabbed her arm again and she huffed as she forced herself to relax and let him have his way.

"This is a little unnecessary, isn't it?" She couldn't stop her mouth from running though, mostly because she wanted to make him feel terrible for how he was treating her. "I mean, you've pointed out plenty of times that I'm some weak little wolf who doesn't stand a chance against you. Are you afraid I'll hurt you?"

He scoffed. "No. Just being precautious."

"Precautious? That's a mighty big word. You sure you know what it means?" She angled her head towards him, regretted it when he stood and she got an eyeful of his crotch. Her gaze zipped to her knees and she wriggled her arms, gritted her teeth and growled as she tested her bonds. The bastard was good at tying people up.

"I know what it means." He moved around her and dropped to his knees, his gaze on her ankles.

Callie kicked him in the chest, knocking him onto his backside, and scowled at him. "That's not necessary!"

Bear growled, flashing huge fangs, the threat enough to have her locking up tight and behaving like a good little wolf.

He got back onto his knees and reached for her left ankle, and she panicked.

"At least tie them together," she blurted, fear getting the better of her again.

His gaze collided with hers.

She knew when he had seen the fear in them, when he had realised why she was afraid of him tying one of her feet to each chair leg, because he averted his gaze, pushed to his feet and tossed the rope over the other chair instead. She breathed a little easier, her panic subsiding as Bear moved away from her, as he made it clear he wouldn't tie her legs.

He rubbed the back of his neck, looked at everything but her, and she could sense the shift in his mood.

And then nothing.

She frowned at him as he went outside, leaving the door open, leaving her alone. How did he shut down his emotions like that? She thought about the tattoo on his nape and had the feeling his past had something to do with it, and also with the way he moved without giving away what he intended to do.

Bear stomped back into the room with an armful of wood, kicked the door closed behind him and sank down in front of the burner. He opened the door, placed the split logs inside, and got the fire going impressively quickly. He closed the door and pushed to his feet, coming to face her.

Firelight chased over him, casting shadows in the valleys between his honed muscles and around his eyes. Making him look every bit as dark and dangerous as she knew him to be.

"Why are you running?"

The same question he had asked her before.

"Can you just take me to your alpha?" She ignored the way his eyebrows knitted hard and fire flashed in his eyes, warning her that he didn't like her questioning him. Or maybe he didn't like that she wanted to meet his leader. "I mean, he can't be any more unreasonable than you."

"Just answer the question, Wolf." He seemed quite determined to keep bringing up the fact she was a wolf.

"Answer my question, Bear." Two could play at that game.

He changed the rules in his favour by coming to loom over her though, forcing her to tilt her head back, his voice dropping to a dangerous whisper.

"You want me to change my mind and tie your legs too?" He glanced down at her right one. "Injury like that might heal tonight, fusing with the rope. That'll hurt."

She glared at him. "You wouldn't."

The thought of having to pull a rope from her flesh sickened her, had her on the verge of answering his question, but she held her tongue. If she responded to his threats, he would keep on threatening her until he got all the answers he wanted. He would use her fear against her.

"I didn't know this was Black Ridge territory. I'm just passing through and I don't want to cause any trouble." She tried to sound calm, but the twist to his lips said she hadn't managed it.

"You're not passing through anywhere. You're running scared and I want to know if I'm about to have a whole troupe of hunters in my pride's territory."

"I told you, I'm not running from Archangel!" She lunged towards him, unable to stop herself as anger and fear flooded her, a heady combination that ripped a reaction from her.

His broad mouth twitched at the corners, as if he wanted to smile. "So you are running then."

She wanted to curse him, wanted to curse herself too for giving that away. "Fine. I'm running. All you need to know is that the ones who are after me aren't hunters. It isn't Archangel. They're not a threat to you—they're a threat to me."

His eyes rapidly darkened.

Made him look as if he wanted to find the ones who were after her and destroy them for her.

She was imagining that, seeing in his expression what she wanted to see, because she had no allies and she badly needed one. She told herself she would have one soon. She would get to the White Wolf pack, and Carrigan wouldn't be able to touch her.

"You going to tell me who is after you?" Bear eased down into a crouch before her.

Callie was tempted to kick him again, even when it wouldn't get her anywhere. "No. I don't answer to you. You can't make me talk."

The cold smile that curved his lips said he could.

He wouldn't.

She searched his eyes, hoping to see in them that he wouldn't hurt her to get answers, but they were blank again, anything he was feeling buried under a layer of ice.

"Take me to your leader." It was a risky move, but it couldn't be worse than being alone in a cabin with Bear. The leader of his pride might be more reasonable, might treat her with a trace of civility and help her. She didn't like bears, but she wasn't dumb enough to turn down help from one. They were powerful, far stronger than wolves. Bear here could probably take on Carrigan and his men alone and decimate them all.

"I'll do just that at daybreak if you haven't answered my questions." His glacial gaze didn't sway from hers, held her fast and chilled her.

He wanted her to believe his leader was more dangerous than he was, which only made her feel that he wasn't. Bear was the attack dog, rabid and wild, running down anything that entered his territory. His alpha was probably a reasonable male in comparison, used Bear as his enforcer rather than getting his own hands bloody.

It was worth the risk.

If it turned out she was wrong, then she would escape and run again.

"Thanks." She eased back in her chair, relaxing and throwing Bear off his game, judging by how his dark eyebrows knitted hard and the corners of his mouth turned downwards.

"For what?"

She canted her head to her left and resisted the temptation to smile sweetly at him. "For letting me know exactly how long I need to be silent. Maybe I can squeeze in a nap. Do you think I have time?"

He scowled at her. "There's a good seven hours between now and dawn. I'll get you talking before then."

"Be a dear and throw another log on the fire. It's so chilly in here." She pretended to shiver, hoping he got that she was taking a jab at his frigid personality.

He huffed and stood, towered over her and stared at her, his eyes revealing nothing. He remained like that for a solid ten minutes or more, until she began to feel uncomfortable and came dangerously close to talking just to break the tense silence.

Just when she thought he would ask her a question, he turned on his heel and walked away from her, yanked the door open and stepped out onto the deck. He stood with his back to her at the edge of the deck and tipped his head back. Looking at the stars? Or maybe asking his ancestors to give him the strength not to kill her. The second one sounded closer to something he might do. She doubted he admired the beauty of the heavens.

He was probably one of those males that didn't see beauty in nature.

Who only saw beauty in things like fighting.

She had met a few wolves like that in her time at the pack, had grown up with two of them. They had laughed at her whenever she had talked about how beautiful the river looked as it sparkled or the sky looked as night fell and the stars emerged one by one. They had mocked her for watching the trout and salmon in the streams or studying hummingbirds and finding them all beautiful, together with nature itself.

They had told her that the only beauty in this world was in the fight. In the breaking of bones. In the shedding of blood. In the battle to live.

Bear struck her as that sort of male.

But as she stared at his back, as she thought about that number someone had inked on his skin, her anger towards him and her prejudices drifted to the back of her mind. There was a small, quiet part of her that whispered she shouldn't judge him so harshly. She didn't know him.

Words rose unbidden, ones that slipped from her despite her best efforts to hold them back.

They fell quietly in the night.

"Were you the eighty-second bear they had captured?"

He turned on a roar.

Slammed the cabin door in her face.

CHAPTER 6

Rune was done with the female.

As dawn broke, painting the sky in hues of orange and pink, and threading the cragged white peaks of the mountains with gold, he finally moved. His legs were stiff from standing on the deck guarding her.

Avoiding her.

He stretched, trying to get some heat back into his cold muscles, refusing to let her see any weakness in him. Her question continued to run around his mind, a handful of words he couldn't shake, despite how badly he wanted to rid himself of them.

Wolf hadn't said a word since then.

She had fallen silent, but she hadn't been asleep. His acute senses had tracked her every movement, his hearing detecting every breath she took. Every sigh. Did she regret pushing him? He didn't care. He told himself that as he opened the cabin door. He didn't care about anything to do with this wolf.

Her gaze instantly landed on him. He growled and flashed fangs at her, and her eyes dropped to her bare knees. He stomped over to her and untied the rope from the chair, almost started untying her wrists too and stopped himself. Wolf could walk to Black Ridge without the use of her hands.

He moved around her.

Felt her gaze on the back of his neck.

Rune turned on her and roared right in her face.

Her shoulders tensed and she curled inwards, angling her body slightly away from him, so her glossy black waves obscured her face. He huffed, denied the urge to apologise to her that ran through him, and strode to the door.

"Move it," he grunted.

"You can't seriously expect me to walk with my hands tied behind my back?"

"Don't need your hands to walk. Just your feet." He refused to look back at her as he reached the deck.

She huffed. "My leg is still healing. What if I trip?"

"Then you'll fall on your fucking face and learn not to trip again." He was being unreasonable. He knew that, and hated it. Something about her pushed all the wrong buttons in him though, and his gut said it wasn't just because she was a wolf.

"Asshole," she bit out. "I'm not going anywhere until you untie me."

He looked over his shoulder at her. The look in her eyes and the mulish twist to her lips said she meant that. She actually thought she could negotiate with him and get him to do what she wanted.

Rune strode back into the cabin, stooped as he reached her and hefted her over his shoulder. "You won't walk, I'll carry you. Won't be comfortable up there."

He accidentally bumped her feet on the back of the chair as he turned with her.

"Son of a bitch." She wriggled against him. As if that was going to make him put her down. With her hands tied behind her back, there wasn't much she could do to hurt him. She angled her head and sank a fang into his right biceps.

Fine, maybe she could hurt him.

He slid her a look. She stilled and released him, her eyes edging to meet his, a flare of regret in them.

"You're right. Making you walk is more of a punishment." He rolled his shoulder and dropped her on her ass.

She grunted as she hit the deck on her back, grimaced and then glared up at him. "Punishment? For what? For accidentally wandering into your damned territory?"

Her eyes slowly widened, understanding dawning in them.

Rune turned away from her before she could say it.

It didn't stop her.

"This is because I asked about that ink on your neck." She grunted and shuffled, and he looked back at her to find her on her knees, pressing her cheek to the wooden boards and trying to lever herself up onto her feet. She huffed and sank against the boards after a few failed attempts, and looked at him. "If I promise not to ask about it again, will you at least help me up?"

He would help her up, but only because some stupid part of him felt bad about the fact he needed to punish her just because she had asked about his ink. She wasn't the first person to ask about it, and she wouldn't be the last. He hadn't reacted badly when people had seen it in the past, or even when they had asked about it.

But for some reason, her asking about it had infuriated him.

Rune strode back to her, bent and grabbed her by the rope that tightly bound her wrists. He pulled her up onto her feet and stared at the rope, waged a war with himself that was over too quickly, the part of him that wanted to keep her bound no match for the side that told him he was being a dick.

He untied the rope.

Seized her wrist before she could sprint off into the woods.

"Don't even think about running." He tightened his grip on her arm. "You run and I *will* chase you."

She looked across at him, her bright amber eyes warmed by the first light of day, made all the more striking by it. "I won't run."

Because she wanted something from his pride, or maybe just Saint. He could see it in her eyes. It irritated him for some reason, made him feel that she would talk to Saint when he got her to Black Ridge, while she insisted on not talking to him. Why wouldn't she talk to him? Sure, he didn't have the same charm Saint had, didn't possess that easy-going and calming air his alpha could put on, but those were hardly reasons for her to refuse to answer Rune's questions.

Maybe it was because she viewed him as a threat.

Or maybe she thought he was incapable of doing whatever it was she thought Saint could do for her.

He huffed at that and started walking, keeping hold of her arm instead of releasing her as he had intended. "Keep up, Wolf."

He didn't care if she didn't want to talk to him, if she didn't want anything to do with him, because he wanted nothing to do with her.

Rune marched her through the forest, heading west, towards Black Ridge. He turned right when he picked up the animal trail, followed a branch of it that led downwards and broadened, forming a path that was wide enough for two people to walk side by side.

After they had been walking for close to an hour, his gaze slid to the wolf. She hadn't complained once about his speed and she had kept up with him despite her injured ankle. She was hobbling badly though, and there was a flicker of pain in her amber eyes whenever she tried to place her weight on her right leg. He glanced down at it and felt like a dick all over again for making her walk on it.

He was no Lowe though.

He wasn't going to carry her through the forest like a princess as Lowe had with his female, Cameo.

He did however slow when he reached a sweeping bend in the track that was now wide enough for three people, one that had been made decades ago by loggers when they had reached this part of the valley. Before Saint had apparently run them off his property. The forest was trying to take back the track, but enough animals used it to keep it serviceable. Rune had caught a few cougars up here in the past—the animal kind—finding them sunning themselves on the dirt. There weren't many places in the forest where the sun could reach the forest floor like it could here.

Rune tugged the wolf to the bend in the trail, where trees had been cut down around a bluff that overlooked the valley. The sun bathed the forest and mountains in golden light, warming the steep granite cliffs of the peaks and softening the green slopes that had formed below them where pebbles and rocks had been washed from those sheer faces.

Wolf stepped past him.

His gaze shifted to her.

Her bright amber eyes darted over everything and she went very still, a predator on the hunt. What was it she was hunting out there? He looked there too, trying to sense whether others were there, the ones she was running from. He couldn't detect anyone out there, but there were a few animals moving around.

"It's beautiful," she breathed, catching his attention.

Rune slid her a look.

"It's beautiful and it's my home. Everything from that side of the valley…" He pointed to the mountains across the basin from him and then swung his arm right. "Up to the glacier is Black Ridge land. Don't be getting ideas about moving in, Wolf."

She looked at him, something in her eyes that he couldn't decipher, that set him on edge.

"What?" he growled.

She shook her head, causing the black waves of her hair to brush her shoulders and catch on the thick material of the fleece she wore. His fleece.

"Nothing. Just… It's odd to hear a male call something beautiful."

He looked at her, a thought rising unbidden, one that instantly had his mood souring.

She was beautiful.

He huffed and turned away from her to glare at the valley. "I call it like I see it."

The valley was beautiful. When he had reached this place after Saint had freed him from the cages, from a dark and lightless existence, he had found this place too beautiful. It hadn't seemed real. It had looked like a dream to him, something impossible, and it wasn't only because it was a stunning valley. It was everything about this place. The wide-open spaces. The air. The sky. The freedom. Everything about this valley had hit him hard, and it had taken him years to grow used to waking up and stepping out of his cabin door to see mountains and forests.

If he could say he was used to it.

Sometimes, he woke in a cold sweat from a nightmare, was convinced he would open his eyes to find himself in a dark cell like the one he had called home in the early days of his captivity, caged with other bear shifters like him, their only light a flickering bulb that the hunters switched on for a few hours a day, when the time of the fights was drawing near.

When he opened his eyes and found aged wood staring back at him, when he hauled his ass out of bed to go to his deck, he was awed by this place all over again. Moved to tears at times.

She would have loved this place.

He rubbed the back of his neck, deeply aware of the ink there.

Saw a flash of another number, marring pale skin splashed with blood.

143-B.

Grace.

Rune squeezed his eyes shut, denying the memories that surged to the surface. When Wolf looked at him and he had the feeling she was going to ask him what was wrong, he grabbed her arm in a bruising grip and pulled her with him towards the trail that cut down through the forest towards the creek.

Opened his eyes and looked at his hand on her wrist as a strange steadiness flowed through him, calming his mind and holding back the images that had started to flood it despite his best attempts to purge them.

What was it about the wolf that made her affect him in ways that left him feeling as if he was spinning, unsteady and off-balance—torn between holding her gently and lashing out at her?

He released her when she looked between his hand on her arm and his face, and he feared she was going to go ahead and ask him what was wrong.

"Keep up." He scoured the route ahead of them, part of his senses locked on her as the rest charted everything in the forest as it closed in around them again.

They had reached a point where the slope became gentler when he sensed movement ahead of him. His senses locked onto it. Not a shifter or a human. An animal.

Rune focused harder on that animal, trying to determine the species of it.

Bear.

“Pick up the pace, Wolf,” Rune growled, backtracked to her and grabbed her arm.

He strode forwards, not regulating his pace this time, uncaring of whether or not Wolf could keep up with him. He needed to see which bear it was.

“You could go a little slower,” the wolf snapped and then muttered, “For a moment there, I thought maybe you had feelings. My bad.”

He bared his teeth at her and kept marching her through the woods. He recognised this place. Water ran somewhere off to his right, trickling and filling the forest with the sound of it as it cut through the dirt and the roots. That stream led to a pool, one that then fed into the creek via another stream that twisted and wound its way down the sloping side of the valley, becoming a small waterfall in places.

Rune’s senses placed the bear at the pool.

He shoved Wolf back against the thick trunk of a pine and glared at her. “Wait here.”

She glared right back at him. “And what if I don’t?”

He narrowed his eyes on hers. “You get to find out what it’s like to be mauled by an angry bear.”

“What is your problem?” She huffed and rolled her eyes, but he knew it was all for show. Her pulse had spiked when he had threatened her, and her fingers trembled slightly as she folded her arms across her chest and gripped the material of the fleece, tugging it into her fists. She gave him a pointed look. “Off you go then. Good riddance. Won’t miss you.”

Rune went to turn away.

She grabbed his arm in a bruising grip, the fierce press of her fingers into his muscles lost on him as her warmth and the softness of her skin hit him hard.

He yanked his arm free of her touch and hissed, “What?”

Her wide eyes held his, darted away from him to scan the forest and then collided with his again. "What is it you're feeling out there? It's not—"

She seemed to gather herself, brought up a barrier around her before he could ask what it was that she feared.

And she did fear something.

He studied her for a moment in which she avoided looking at him, affected an air that said she wasn't bothered by anything when his senses said otherwise. He had shaken her when he had threatened her, but whoever was out there, after her, terrified her.

"It's a bear." Those words slipped from him and when she looked at him, worry shimmering in her eyes, he couldn't stop himself from adding, "The animal kind."

She sank against the tree, a blush burning up her cheeks as she looked at her bare feet again. Ashamed she had been afraid of a little bear? She didn't need to be. She hadn't known what was out there and she was running from someone. It was perfectly reasonable of her to assume that it was her enemy out there, close to her.

He looked at her, the soft part of him that should have died long ago rising to the fore, making him want to ask if she was going to be all right if he left her here alone. He shut it down. It was no concern of his whether she was going to be fine without him. She meant nothing to him. He didn't know her and he didn't want to know her.

He stormed away before his irritating need to ask her if she was fine won and pushed the words from him.

As the distance between them grew, that softer part of him faded to the background, vanquished again by the side that had kept him alive for decades, had helped him survive a living hell.

But the moment he spotted the bear ahead of him and caught her scent, the soft part of him rose like a monster to obliterate all trace of hardness in him.

The reason he had wanted Wolf to keep her distance.

He didn't want her seeing this side of him and he had known it would come to the fore if the bear was one he knew.

Loved.

The female black bear stopped drinking from the wide pool in the clearing and lifted her head, her dark eyes settling on him as her head swung his way.

Misty.

His heart clenched when he looked around the clearing and found no sign of a cub. He looked back at her, hating how lean she looked. Last year must have been hard on her. He hadn't seen her for a good part of summer into autumn, had been concerned about her, and it turned out he'd had good reason to be worried.

He eased into a crouch and opened his arms to her.

She ambled over to him, grunting and moaning, playful sounds that were her way of greeting him. He moaned back at her, dropped to his knees as she reached him and wrapped his arms around her. He smiled as she nudged him with her head, as she wriggled and wanted to play with him, trying to initiate a wrestling match.

Just as she had when she had been a cub with her sister, Brook.

Gods, those had been good days. He had devoted himself to caring for the twin cubs, had loved watching them growing up, seeing them getting stronger.

He weathered a few gentle nips from Misty as he tried to ease her back so he could get a good look at her, huffed when she wasn't interested in playing by his rules. She moaned and placed her front paws onto his thighs, rubbed her head against his, her fur tickling him.

Rune wrapped his arms around her neck and ruffled her fur, knowing what she wanted from him. She always had been the more love-hungry of the two sisters.

When he tried to ease her back again this time, she let him. He ran an assessing gaze over her. She was thin, needed to fatten up after her winter sleep.

"You should swing by Black Ridge. Come get some food." He stroked her right ear and smiled when she licked the wound on his left forearm, the one Wolf had made with her fangs. "Yeah, I got into another fight. I'm good though. Let's talk about you. Brook has been by already. She has a little boy in tow."

Rune tried to harden his heart when he looked at Misty, soul-deep aware that the two sisters were getting old now and that last year's offspring might have been the last for her.

Misty stiffened and Rune wanted to growl as he honed his senses on the forest around him.

And realised the wolf had moved, had disobeyed his orders and had followed him.

He glared over his shoulder at her, keeping one hand in Misty's fur to calm her.

Wolf's amber eyes shifted to the bear and she risked a step closer.

Rune wanted to growl when Misty relaxed, irritation swift to flood him. She shouldn't be so calm around a stranger. It was dangerous. Not everyone who passed through Black Ridge land was a friend of his and the pride's. He looked at the bear, wanted to chastise her for lowering her guard, but then it struck him that she had good reason to be calm around the wolf.

Wolf was with him and she was wearing his fleece, smelled like him to Misty.

"Do you often stop to talk to animals?" Wolf cast a curious look between him and Misty.

She made him sound like Doctor Dolittle.

"Not often. Misty here is an exception." He smoothed her black fur, roughed it up a little, and held back his smile as she slapped a big wet kiss on his cheek, licking it. "I'll always stop for a chat with her or Brook."

Wolf eyed him closely, the look in her eyes warning him that she was in danger of changing her mind about him, that she had spotted that tiny seed of softness within him—a seed he had wanted to keep hidden from her.

He could see in those eyes that she wanted to mention he had feelings, ones she had thought him incapable of just minutes ago, and when she opened her mouth he expected her to call him on that.

Only a single word tumbled from her rosy lips.

"Why?"

CHAPTER 7

Rune's first instinct was to tell the wolf it was none of her damned business, but she moved another step closer to him and Misty stiffened. Her uneasiness hit him hard as she moaned and swayed, her dark eyes locked on the wolf. When the sow hit him, slapping her right paw against his left forearm and catching him with her long claws, Rune knew better than to seize hold of her to stop her.

Instead, he turned on the wolf. "Back off. If you back off, I'll tell you."

She surprised him by moving back several steps, placing more distance between them, revealing how badly she wanted to know why he was being gentle with this bear, why he would gladly take the time to speak with her or spend time with her whenever they crossed paths. He didn't like the thought of revealing anything personal to this female, but he was a man of his word.

The apprehension he could feel in Misty subsided and he carefully lifted his left hand. Before he could rub her fur with it to show her that she was safe, the sow huffed and nudged his forearm, licked the cuts she had made.

"It's okay. Nothing to feel bad about. Wolf scared you." He let Misty assuage her guilt by cleaning the welts in his arm and looked back over his shoulder at the wolf. Was he really going to do this?

She had accused him of having no feelings, and he was about to show her that he had more than he wanted, that there was a side of him that could feel the same soft and weak emotions she did.

He huffed.

"I raised Misty and her twin sister Brook." He wondered if he could leave it at that, but the look in Wolf's eyes said she wanted to know more. "Has to be fifteen… maybe seventeen years ago now."

"I didn't know wild bears lived that long." Her gaze flicked to Misty, a hint of concern in it, as if she was worried about the bear hitting old age too.

Rune grunted, "I've known ones that lived longer than thirty years."

But secretly, he was worried that Misty wouldn't reach that grand old age.

He tried to shut out the presence of the wolf and focus on Misty, wrangled his feelings as he rubbed her scruff, trying to shut down the part of him that was making his throat feel tight and his chest constrict as he looked at the black bear sow.

When she looked at him, he saw her as she had been all those years ago, a young and rebellious cub who had wanted to play non-stop, who had kept him awake most nights by demanding food, and who had been the boss out of the twins.

His eyes misted and he cleared his throat, part of him wanting to snap and roar at the wolf behind him as the feel of her gaze on him heated his back.

"Follow," he murmured to Misty, stroked her right ear and stood. He moved a few steps away from her, in the direction of Black Ridge, and thankfully she obeyed him and began following him.

She kept pace with him, rummaging in the greenery at times, wandering left and right a few feet but never straying too far.

The wolf followed him too, keeping pace with him but keeping her distance. She remained mercifully silent as she watched him with Misty, said nothing even when he knew she probably wanted to. She had a lot of ammunition she could use against him now and he was surprised she wasn't taking this opportunity to throw some snarky comments in his direction.

"There's berries in the freezer," Rune husked to Misty as she ambled along beside him, swaying to nudge his right leg from time to time. He snorted when she nipped at his jeans, still trying to make him play with her. Maybe he would later, once she was fed and Wolf was gone. "I picked a whole bunch last year just for you. I'm going to make you so fat and then I'll make a nice place for you to rest."

He knew he shouldn't interfere in nature, that what he was doing was trying to tame her—cage her—but he needed to look after her.

He didn't want to cage her. That wasn't what he was doing. He just wanted to be a good foster parent for her. If she stayed at Black Ridge, she would be safe and would have all the food she needed, and she would live longer. She would be free to come and go as she pleased, but that soft part of him hoped she would choose to hang out at the Ridge for most of the year.

"How did you come to raise bear cubs?" Wolf's gaze drilled into his back, silently pressing him to answer that question and tell her more about his relationship with the bear, just as he had promised.

"Hunters killed their mother." He tried to keep it at that, but the memory of that day hit him hard and had him growling, "The spineless bastards targeted her during her winter sleep. Killed her for no godsdamned reason, leaving her cubs without a mother."

"So you took them in," she whispered softly, making him want to look at her and not want to look at her at the same time.

He didn't want to see the look that would accompany those words, feared it might put a dent in the barrier around his heart.

He nodded and looked at Misty.

She was like a daughter to him.

Both her and Brook were.

They finally reached the creek, a section of it where it was broad and shallow, running swiftly in the deepest part of it. At the edges, boulders that had been brought down the mountain caused it to slow. Trees lined the bank on both sides, providing a contrast to the bubbling pale blue water. This wasn't going to be fun. When water was that colour, it was because it was coming down off the glacier, was filled with minerals and sediment, which meant he was in for a chilly crossing.

Misty groaned as she patted the water.

Rune looked down at her. "Yeah, it's cold. Blame the glacier for that. A little too swift for you too. Come on."

He stooped, removed his boots and tied the laces together, and then pulled off his socks and stuffed them inside. He slung the boots over his left shoulder and scooped the bear into his arms, and looked back at the wolf. She gave him a look, one he could easily read. He shrugged. He was more than happy carrying the bear. He just hadn't wanted to carry her.

"Don't expect the same treatment." He waded into the water, the coldness of it instantly sapping his warmth and making his muscles stiff.

The current was stronger than he had anticipated in the middle where it reached just above his knees, and he had to be careful about each step he took, placing his foot and ensuring his footing was good before he moved his weight to it. If he slipped, Misty would get a dousing and might even be swept downstream. Gods, the thought of her getting hurt because he had failed to look after her was like a hot knot in his gut, twisting ever tighter as he slowly navigated the river.

Relief poured through him when he reached the point where the water slowed again, growing shallower, and he could see his feet. He picked his way around the rocks and smooth boulders to the earth bank and set Misty down.

He dumped his boots and untied the laces.

"Um." The wolf sounded worried.

Rune looked back at her and found her standing at the edge of the deeper water, her amber eyes locked on it, worry written plainly across every sculpted line of her face.

"What's the hold up?" The softer part of him called him a dick for asking that question when he could see what the problem was.

She was sporting an injured leg. The cold water alone would make it hard for her to cross the stream, sapping her strength even further. If he added the current in the deeper water and the fact she couldn't see where she was placing her feet, she was liable to end up downstream or drowned.

He huffed and forgot his boots, gave Misty a look that told her to remain where she was. "Stay."

Misty ambled into the bushes.

Rune sighed, shook his head and crossed the creek again. When he reached the wolf, he hefted her over his shoulder and banded his arm around her thighs, keeping her in place as she grunted. He turned with her and began back across the river.

"You couldn't carry me in a nicer way?" She shoved her hands against his back, pushing herself up as she muttered, "This isn't comfortable."

"It isn't meant to be comfortable. It's meant to get you from A to B." He grimaced as he placed a foot wrong, skidded a little and almost fell into the water.

He blamed the wolf for that. Talking to her was distracting him. The difficulty he was having concentrating had nothing to do with how warm she was against him or how the fleece she wore had ridden up and his bare arm was in contact with her very bare thighs.

"You didn't carry Misty like she was garbage," she bit out, sounding genuinely offended that he had slung her over his shoulder in a fireman's carry.

"Misty is a princess. She gets carried like one." He grinned, purely because she couldn't see it, and waited for her to hit him with a sarcastic or biting comeback.

He felt disappointed when she didn't.

Felt angry at himself too.

He was getting too comfortable around her. He shouldn't be wanting to hear her snarky retorts, shouldn't be hungry to have her snapping something amusing at him, something that revealed her interesting sense of humour and that strength he had seen in her—the one that said she could take on the world if she had to.

Rune shifted his grip to closer to her knees when they reached the shallower water, preparing to set her down.

His entire body stiffened when she tilted forwards and pulled him backwards, yanked a reaction from him in a heartbeat as something inside him roared at him to stop her from plunging headfirst into the icy water.

He grabbed her.

Froze.

Wolf locked up tight too, her heartbeat off the scale.

And then she was battering his back, punching him in his damned kidney.

"You freaking pervert!" She elbowed him in the back of his head, jerking it forwards.

At this point, he was sure sense should have kicked in and made him remove his hand from the peachy softness of her bare backside.

Only it didn't.

He stood there like an idiot, reeling from the feel of her warm skin against his palm.

Good gods.

It made him too aware of how close that part of her was to his face, how she was bare beneath his fleece. She elbowed him again, harder this time, the force of her blow enough to knock that sense he was lacking into him.

He was quick to stride to the edge of the river and set her down, averted his gaze as she hurried to cover herself, something he found strange since she had stood naked before him last night and hadn't cared then.

A noble part of him that he hadn't realised still existed until that moment pushed him to apologise.

He lifted his head to do just that.

Staggered backwards as he got a fist in his mouth as his reward.

The coppery tang of blood flooded his mouth, made him growl and square up to her.

"It was an accident. I was stopping you from falling!" He stepped right up to her, until there was barely an inch between them, and glared down at her. "You want to take a dive into glacier water?"

Her lips flattened, fire blazing in her eyes as she held his gaze. Rose climbed her cheeks and he didn't think it was because she was furious with him. He told himself to be the gentleman, told himself not to mention that her mouth might have been saying one thing to him back in the river, but her body had been saying something else.

He had been close enough to scent it on her.

She had liked the feel of his hand on her backside.

And it had rattled her.

Hell, it had rattled him too.

"I wasn't taking liberties," he muttered and turned away from her, tugged his boots on and laced the first one. "Like I'd want a wolf."

She growled and kicked him in the hip while he was bent over, easily knocked him off-balance and onto his ass. He bared fangs at her. She didn't back down, didn't flinch away. She stood there with that fire in her eyes, fury he had ignited in her.

"I don't know what your problem is with wolves… but if I had to guess, I'd have to go with you being the crux of it. Your shitty personality is enough to put any wolf in a bad mood."

She hobbled away from him and he scowled at her back, tempted to tell her why he had a problem with her kind. He kept his mouth shut, because he didn't want her to know about him and he didn't care whether she hated him.

He didn't care that she was angry with him.

He really didn't.

He huffed and tracked her with his senses, keeping tabs on her as he finished tying his boots, in case she got ideas about running or finding a really heavy branch to hit him with. She stomped around the woods, muttering to herself.

Misty came to him and nudged him, and he stroked her black fur.

Grumbled, "Yeah, she's got a bad attitude… but she's probably got her reasons. We all do."

He got to his feet and patted Misty's scruff, silently telling her to follow him. He trudged into the forest and found the wolf sitting on a fallen, rotting log, huffing as she checked her leg.

"Is it all right?" he said.

She shot him a look that asked what did he care?

He sighed. "You were going to fall."

She looked as if she was going to argue again and then her expression shifted, growing defeated with a hint of regretful as she muttered, "I know. It just… When you… It's…"

She blew out her breath.

Closed her eyes.

Lowered her head.

"In the past, at—" She cut herself off.

Rune stared at her, his senses locked on her, revealing something to him that had him backing down, dulled the edge of his mood and had guilt flaring in his stomach.

Fear.

Hurt.

He didn't need to be a genius to piece it together. This wolf had some bad experiences in her past, had been subjected to abuse, and his touch had triggered memories of that time.

"Sorry," he mumbled.

She shook her head but didn't look at him.

When she drew in a breath, it was shaky.

Rune had heard tales of how some wolf packs treated females, had seen with his own eyes at the compound that those tales were true. Wolf males had a bad tendency to think they could do as they pleased with the females of their kind. He had taught them to treat the females with more respect, had entered into more than one fight outside the ring to teach the wolves a lesson about how a female should be treated.

She pushed to her feet. Dusted her backside down. Hobbled to him, but kept her eyes on the ground.

"Forget about it."

Rune tracked her as she walked past him. He couldn't do that. The thought of such a beautiful female, such a strong female, being treated like that had an inferno running through his veins, made him want to hunt down every male who had hurt her and butcher them.

He patted Misty again and started after the wolf, easily caught up with her before she took a wrong turn and gently caught her arm. He led her back towards the river and picked up the trail that ran parallel to it and would take them to the Ridge. Once she was on that path, he released her again but kept his senses locked on her, making sure she couldn't move a muscle without him knowing about it.

The trees began to thin and he smelled smoke, and frying bacon.

Black Ridge.

His stomach growled in response to the tempting smell that evoked images of fresh soft white rolls thickly stacked with the breakfast meat.

"Was that your mouth or your stomach?" The wolf sounded brighter.

He wasn't glad about that.

He wasn't.

"Stomach. I missed out on dinner last night. Steaks and beer." He looked over his shoulder at her. "Had to save a wolf."

She frowned at him, that mulish twist to her lips again. "I would have gotten myself out of that snare eventually."

"Yeah," he grunted. "And lost a foot in the process. You don't have to thank me."

"I won't," she bit out.

"Good." He refused the temptation to glance at her again.

"Good," she parroted.

Almost tugging another smile from him.

He shut down the urge and stoked his mood, reminded himself that she was a wolf. A beautiful wolf, but still a wolf. He couldn't trust her. For all he knew, she was probably manipulating him right that moment, was probably close to completing her mission to reveal the location of Black Ridge to Archangel, pleasing her masters.

That thought shoved him straight into a bad mood, had him skipping all the stages in between what had been a rather good mood and a black need to hunt and kill whoever was out there, looking for this wolf.

The clearing of Black Ridge came into view and he was tempted to drive her away, to turn her around and march her back into the woods before she could see it. He held his nerve and kept striding forwards, because he still had questions he wanted answers to and part of him wanted to see what would happen.

If the wolf was working with hunters, then they were about to make a fatal mistake in targeting his pride.

He would rip them apart with his bare hands.

Rune stepped out into the morning sunshine, leaving the chill of the shady forest behind, and smiled as Misty lumbered towards the pebbly bank of the creek. The water was shallower here, remained that way throughout Black Ridge and even as it passed Cougar Creek, the neighbouring property. It was barely a foot or two deep, so he didn't worry about the bear.

His smile widened as he watched her frolicking at the edge of the water, chasing what was probably a fish, acting as if she was young again.

When he passed her, he muttered, "Come on."

Misty broke away from the bank and bounded past him, nipped at his calf, hard enough that it stung. He sighed and turned his head, tracked her with his gaze until she stopped and looked towards the heart of Black Ridge.

Rune looked there too.

The five cabins situated in the grassy clearing on this side of the creek looked warm and inviting in the sunshine, the logs all deep shades of amber that reminded him of the wolf's eyes. His gaze skipped over the two cabins nearest him, both of which stood with their backs to him, the gable ends and the decks facing south, towards the other three cabins.

He spotted what Misty had just as the bear began running.

Maverick.

The black-haired male was wringing out washing near the creek a short distance from his cabin, the one on the left of the two Rune was closing in on now. He paused and his head swung towards Rune, his grey eyes catching on Misty instead as she hurried towards him, her bushy backside wiggling with each rushed step.

Maverick cracked a rare grin.

Opened his arms and caught Misty as she barrelled into him, rolled onto his back with her on top of him and growled as he playfully wrestled with her.

Rune huffed. "Hussy. Always running off after that grizzly."

Maverick eased up into a sitting position as Misty swatted at him, caught her in a light chokehold as his eyes landed on Rune and then the wolf trailing behind him. His friend nodded towards her.

"Bringing in strays now?"

Rune shook his head. "Where's Saint?"

"Cougar Creek." Maverick rubbed Misty's fur, appeasing the bear as she kept trying to initiate play, keeping his eyes on the wolf. "Was worried about you there for a moment, Rune. You good?"

Rune grunted. "Just fantastic."

He was deeply aware of the female tailing him as he looked at his friend and noticed the lines that bracketed his mouth and the dull edge to his grey eyes, signs that the male had been up all night worrying about him. The need to apologise to him was strong, but he pushed it aside and swore he would do it later, once the two of them were alone.

Wolf growled, "Cougar Creek? Please tell me you don't mean cougar like shifters?"

He nodded towards the south, beyond Saint's cabin where it stood proud in the centre of the clearing, not far from a sweeping bend in the stream. "Down that way. Be good or I'll feed you to them."

She scowled at him, her eyes brightening.

Hell, he wasn't happy either. He had been banking on Saint being here to question her, taking her off his hands. He had thought that when he got her to Black Ridge, he would be done with her and wouldn't have to see her anymore.

"Get Misty some berries from the freezer," he said to Maverick and was tempted to growl at him when he just carried on staring at the wolf. "Maverick?"

Maverick slid his grey eyes to Rune. "Sure."

Rune grabbed hold of the wolf's arm before Maverick could start staring at her again and marched her past his friend's cabin towards the one beside it.

"Where are you taking me now?" she bit out.

Rune looked across at her.

"It's time you answered my questions."

CHAPTER 8

Rune marched the wolf up the steps to the raised deck of his cabin and opened the door for her. He pushed her inside and closed the door behind him, released her and bent to remove his boots as she wandered deeper into his home. Bringing her into his cabin was a mistake, he knew it, but the alternative had been keeping her outside where Maverick could see her.

And for some godsdamned reason, he had needed to get her away from that male.

Her amber eyes darted over everything, which was to say it darted over his worn green couch, the unlit log burner that stood against the left wall near it, and what amounted to a sink and two cabinets by the window that overlooked the deck.

He had never gotten around to furnishing his cabin, that part of him that still expected Saint to wise up and change his mind about Rune being a member of the pride telling him not to bother getting too comfortable.

His loft bedroom was a shining example of how deeply he expected Saint to kick him out of the pride.

He didn't even have a bed frame up there. His bed was a double mattress placed directly on the floorboards.

Still, it was leagues better than his previous accommodation, which had resembled the prison cell it was—white concrete walls, a trough in the corner that passed as a toilet, and a thin mattress tossed directly on the floor, because even bolting down a metal frame wouldn't stop a shifter from ripping it right up and using it on the mortals holding them.

Gods, the number of times he had fantasised about killing them.

An impenetrable layer of toughened glass had been the door of his cell, controlled by electronics, and anyone who had gotten too frisky had been hit with a dose of gas to knock them out and teach them that trying to rise up against their captors was a bad idea.

The humans had taken every precaution when handling them too. Rune still had nightmares about his collar. He rubbed his throat, trying to suppress the memories that crowded his mind. He had hated the collar more than the fights. The hunters had been ingenious, embracing technology as mankind had discovered it, adding things to what had started out as a plain, two-inch-thick steel collar. At the press of a button, his captors had been able to take him down.

He had lost count of the number of times they had used it to keep him in line.

The sharp stab of a needle in his neck to drug him if he disobeyed. A few thousand volts blasted through him if he really misbehaved. The size of the collar alone had stopped him from being able to shift while wearing it.

The only time they had removed it was in the cage.

Another press of a button had released it and given him a taste of freedom and he had been quick to make good use of it against whoever had been in the cage with him.

Partly because he had needed an outlet for his pent-up aggression, and partly because the more non-humans he maimed or killed in the ring, the more lenient the hunters had been on him. A good victory that had left the customers satisfied had often been enough to score him several days of being allowed to wander the halls and use the gym and visit the canteen as often as he had wanted.

When Maverick had been captured, Rune had taken him under his wing and taught him how to get as much freedom as he could while still being held in a compound. Maverick had taken to killing a little too well, was a naturally aggressive male who hadn't baulked at the bloodshed or sobbed himself to sleep like so many of the other captives. Together, they had risen in status, had gained the respect of most of the shifters in their area of the compound.

And by the time Saint had rescued them, the hunters had given them free run of the place, never bothering to keep them in their cells outside of a few hours a day, letting them go about their business.

Mostly because Maverick had developed a tendency to keep every male in line. The slightest scuffle broke out and he would be there, in the thick of the fight, whether it was between two immortals or an immortal and a human guard. The shifters had learned not to fight when he was around.

"Are you even listening to me, Rune?" A high and haughty female voice dragged him back to the present, and he glared at the wolf as he straightened.

"No." He kicked his boots aside. "And I don't appreciate you using my name."

She glared right back at him for that.

He was going to have words with Maverick later about the fact he had revealed his name to the wolf. He hadn't wanted her to know it, hadn't wanted that level of familiarity between them. She had no need to know his name and he had no need to know hers.

"Callie." She tossed that at him on a black look. "There. Now you know mine and we're even. Is that better?"

He grunted at her, was close to growling as he cursed her in his mind. "No."

She folded her arms across her chest. "Look. I'm guessing Saint is your alpha and he's not here, so just let me go. I just need to get to the White Wolf pack. I know their lodge is near here."

"White Wolf?" Rune scowled at her now. "What business do you have with them? Is that your pack?"

"No. I'm..." Her gaze drifted to the log burner as she rubbed her arm through the black fleece. "I don't have a pack right now."

Rune moved to the log burner and Callie shuffled back a few steps, keeping the distance between them steady. She placed the end of the green couch between them and gripped the back of it with one hand as he crouched and built a fire to take the morning chill out of the air inside the cabin.

"Why don't you have a pack?" He wasn't going to waste the opportunity to get her to answer more questions. He told himself the reason he needed to know that wasn't because he wanted to know more about her but because it might reveal who was after her and why she was on his pride's land.

She gave a little shrug. "I'm just between packs."

She was a terrible liar.

"Why do you want to go to White Wolf then?" He lit the kindling and waited for the flames to catch before closing the door.

When he rose to his feet and looked at her, he thought she might shrug that question off too, but then she sighed and stared beyond him, out of the window near the door.

"I need to get to Rourke. Rourke can protect me."

Rourke?

Rune wanted to growl at just the name, really wanted to growl when he tried to imagine what kind of male would go with it.

"Protect you from what?" he bit out, a little harder than intended, and she tensed and her gaze darted to him.

The look in her eyes said she wasn't going to answer that question. "I just need to get to Rourke."

Rune turned to face her and folded his arms across her chest, mirroring her posture. "You think this Rourke can protect you from whatever you're running from?"

"I don't think. I know he can." She held his gaze, unflinching even when he growled at her.

"So who is after you?" Rune wanted to know the answer to that question most of all, pretended the sudden spark of anger that lit his blood on fire was all about that rather than how Callie kept talking about this Rourke male as if he was some kind of white knight for her. "I want to know who the hell is in this valley, liable to be crossing into my territory."

"*Your* territory?" She canted her head, her dark eyebrows knitting hard. "I thought it was Saint's territory?"

"It's Black Ridge territory," he snarled, losing patience. "Extends from here to the glacier… and I have a right to know who is in it when they're a threat to my pride. Like you."

Her eyes widened and her mouth flapped open and then snapped closed. The fire in her eyes that had dulled as he had tossed that accusation at her flared back up again, burning brighter than ever.

"I'm not a threat to your pride." She looked close to stomping her foot or clawing his eyes out.

"I'll decide that. You crossed into these lands uninvited and bringing trouble on your tail. Had enough of that happening in recent months, so I want to know… who the hell is out there!" His mood faltered, took a swift dark turn as the thought of his pride in trouble again had him spiralling, roused a fierce need to protect his friends. "I'm still not convinced I'm not about to hear a chopper circling overhead and have Archangel soldiers rappelling into the fucking clearing."

Her eyes shot wide again, and she growled this time as she narrowed them on him, her anger hitting him hard as it rolled off her, pushed his bear side and agitated it, flooding him with a need to fight.

"I told you I'm not with Archangel and it isn't Archangel who are after me. But fine… don't believe me. When no hunters show up, you'll have to believe that." She hobbled towards the back of the couch, keeping it between them.

When she didn't stop, kept on limping towards the front of the cabin, Rune barked, "Where do you think you're going?"

She tossed him daggers. "I'm leaving. Honestly, I should have known better. I'll find the White Wolf pack myself. At least now I know it isn't in this valley."

She had thought the wolves lived in this place? Not a chance. He wanted to laugh at her for her mistake, but a flash of her desperately trying to chew her way out of a snare and how afraid she had been at times hit him hard, silencing him. She was running scared, had probably taken a wrong turn somewhere, and now she was paying for it by having to deal with him.

Rune stepped into her path. "You're not going anywhere, Wolf."

"Callie. My name is Callie." Fire blazed hotter in her eyes, making them glow like an inferno, and rather than backing away from him, she squared up to him.

Brave little wolf, but foolish too. It was dangerous to incite him, even more dangerous to challenge him. His bear side had a hard time differentiating between an enemy and someone who was just pissed at him when it felt challenged, usually ended up viewing everyone as a threat and someone to fight.

He backed off a step as he wrestled with himself and bared his fangs when a light filled her eyes, one that said she thought she had scored a victory, had been the one to make him back off.

"Believe me, Wolf, the only reason I'm backing off is because you're dangerously close to getting yourself hurt. I'm one bear you don't provoke." He flexed his fingers and stared her down, his fangs flashing between his lips as he ground out each word, as he battled the urge to shift and put her in her place.

Never.

He wouldn't hurt a female.

Couldn't.

It was a line he wouldn't cross.

Her throat worked on a hard swallow and she moved back a step. Her gaze darted to the window and then back to him, and she stroked her left arm with her right hand, lightly rubbing it.

Her brow furrowed. "Look. I just want to get to Rourke."

"Enough with this Rourke guy!" Rune snapped.

The door behind him opened and the earthy scent of Saint hit him, together with the feel of his alpha's eyes on the back of his head. Rune could feel the silent command in that look, the order to back down and explain what was happening.

Rune curled his fingers into fists and stared at Callie, seething with a need to lash out at her, to make her talk and make her forget the wolf she kept mentioning.

Her amber eyes shifted from him to Saint. "Are you the alpha here?"

"I am." Saint's deep voice rolled over Rune, calm and commanding, the sound of it easing some of the tension from him. Saint moved to stand beside him and placed his left hand on Rune's right shoulder.

That touch was enough to have him backing down because it told him that his alpha was here now and he would deal with things.

Rune released the breath he had been holding and twisted away from Callie and Saint, breaking free of his hold. He paced to the far end of the small cabin, needing some space and some air.

"I need to get to the White Wolf pack. I need to get to Rourke." Her softly spoken words curled around Rune and worked strange magic on him to calm him further, until she mentioned the wolf again.

"Again with Rourke," he muttered and felt Saint glance at him.

"Rourke is the alpha at the White Wolf Lodge. The white wolf himself. I know him." Saint's dark gaze landed on him again and lingered this time, and when Rune looked at him, he didn't like how closely the male was watching him, as if he was trying to figure out what was wrong with him. Saint scrubbed a hand over his dark beard in a thoughtful way as his eyebrows lowered. "I think you might have met him once. Tall, good-looking male with white hair."

Rune grunted, his mood souring further at that, as the picture he had in his head, one he was mentally pummelling, turned into a male with Hollywood looks that made even Lowe and Knox look average.

"They live in the valley next door." Saint lifted his right arm, his black-and-blue checked fleece shirt stretching tight over his biceps and across his broad shoulders, and pointed towards the mountains east of the Ridge, where Rune had found Callie.

She didn't look happy when she glanced over her shoulder and then at Saint.

"I was close to reaching them?" Her gaze leaped to Rune and darkened. "I could have reached them by now. I could have been safe."

"Safe? From what?" Saint frowned at her.

"She won't tell me. She's running from something but she won't tell me what. Keeps insisting it's not Archangel though." Rune strode back towards Saint, his eyes locked on her as he ran a hand over his head, just the feel of how closely shorn his hair was hurling him back to his time in captivity.

The bastards had always loved shaving the heads of those they held in the compounds, and while Maverick had managed to shake off the habit of having his hair barely two or three millimetres in length, Rune had gotten too used to it.

Anything longer than that irritated him.

Another change in his personality he couldn't shake, no matter how hard he tried.

Callie scowled at him. "It's not Archangel. It's other wolves. Is there a way to the valley from this one?"

Rune looked at her bruised and bloodied ankle. She wasn't trekking anywhere with that injury. He lifted his eyes to meet hers again. They shone with determination, with courage he had seen in too many eyes in his time. It never lasted. As soon as things got tough, as soon as it started to hurt too much, that courage would crumble and she would give up.

"Rune can drive you to the White Wolf pack." Saint refused to look at him when Rune's gaze darted to him.

"Hell, no," Rune snapped. "I'm done with her. She can make her own way there."

Saint slid him a look that said he hadn't been giving Rune a choice. Rune wanted to fight his alpha on it, didn't want to be near Callie now that he had done his duty and had brought her to Saint, but in the end he huffed and stomped away from him.

Muttered, "Fine."

"Thank you." Callie's soft voice lured his focus to her. He looked over his shoulder at her and found her looking at him rather than Saint. Her gaze shifted back to the big brunet male. "You don't know how much this means to me. Rourke can protect me from Carrigan."

Rune stiffened, every muscle clamping down on his bones, as that name hit his ears.

Carrigan.

That was the manufactured perfume he had scented on her trail—on her. That was why he had been so agitated around her at first, driven to lash out at her and hurt her.

Because she had smelled like that traitor.

Saint scratched his dark beard as his expression shifted towards pensive and Rune knew he was trying to think of where he knew that name from. He also knew the moment the big brunet bear remembered it, because Saint slid him a worried look.

Rune curled his fingers into fists and clenched them so hard that his bones ached and burned, trying to tamp down the urge to lash out at everything in the vicinity as he thought about that wretched male being in the same valley as he was.

"What's wrong?" Callie looked from him to Saint and back again.

"Nothing." Saint smiled, an easy one that disarmed the wolf. He stepped towards her and looked her over, concern creasing his brow. "We should be able to get you some clothes. The females here might have something that will fit you. I'll ask around. In the meantime, you should rest that ankle."

She nodded and relaxed a little, but then her expression grew awkward and she fidgeted with the sleeve of the black fleece she wore.

"Spit it out," Rune grunted, aware she wanted to ask for something and was nervous about doing it.

Saint wasn't liable to turn her down. Besides, Rune wanted to know what she was lacking now. Saint was offering her clothes and an escort, everything she could possibly need.

She scowled at him and then her features softened as she looked back at Saint. "I don't suppose breakfast is out of the question?"

Breakfast. Just the thought of the bacon he had smelled when coming into the clearing had him salivating and his stomach close to rumbling again. It hadn't even crossed his mind that she might be as starving as he was.

"I'll get Lowe to bring some over for you." Saint offered her another easy smile.

Rune resisted the temptation to growl at his alpha as a need surged through him, one he instantly kicked to the curb, because he didn't want to be the one to bring her breakfast. He didn't want to be on the receiving end of a smile from her or a look that told him she was grateful to him.

He didn't want to please her.

When Saint turned to leave, Rune followed him and closed the door behind them as they stepped out onto the deck. He caught Saint's arm before he could move off the bottom step and the male looked back at him.

Rune warred with himself as he looked into Saint's deep brown eyes and saw in them that his alpha was waiting, aware of what he was going to suggest. The fact that Saint knew him so well made him feel like a callous bastard, something close to the same brand of wretched as Carrigan was, because he was also about to betray someone to get something he wanted.

No.

This wasn't a betrayal. Not really. Not in the way Carrigan had operated. The wolf had been a cage fighter too, but had quickly learned to suck up to the humans who had been running the arena, gaining favour with them by snitching on the activities of the other immortals.

Rune had paid a terrible price because of Carrigan, and he owed the male for what he had done to him.

And to Grace.

"She's done nothing wrong, Rune." Saint's deep voice swept around him and Rune almost buckled, almost decided against doing what he felt he needed to do.

Almost.

He owed Carrigan though, and if he could hurt the male by taking something he loved from him, he would do it.

Only he didn't just intend to hurt Carrigan by taking Callie to the White Wolf pack and Rourke, placing her under the protection of a powerful pack. He intended to lure the male into a trap and kill the bastard.

"I need closure, Saint. You know what Carrigan did to me. You know what he did to Grace. I can't… I'll never be able to move on with my life until I bury that part of my past." Rune ran a hand over his close-cropped hair again and huffed. "I won't hurt her, but I also won't drive her to the wolves. I want to lure Carrigan out. I need to deal with him."

Saint's dark eyes searched his for the longest time, so long that Rune felt sure the male was going to put his foot down and order him to drive Callie to the White Wolf pack and to forget about getting revenge on Carrigan.

But then the big bear heaved a sigh.

Held Rune's gaze, the look in his eyes warning Rune not to lose his head in the heat of the moment.

And turned away from him, breaking free of his hold.

"Just make sure she isn't caught in the crossfire. I don't need Rourke and a pack of angry wolves coming to bite my ass."

CHAPTER 9

Callie rose from the green couch when the door to her left opened and Rune stepped back into the room. It felt too small as he glanced at her, the way their eyes collided seeming to suck the air from her lungs. What was it about this bear that made him affect her so badly?

She didn't think it was fear. She wasn't scared of him, not when he was like this anyway. Maybe not even when he growled and roared and tried to frighten her. Whenever he acted like that, she reacted in the same way, wanted to bare fangs and stand up to him. She was starting to think she had a death wish she hadn't known about until she had met Rune.

Why else would she want to provoke a powerful and dangerous bear?

He closed the door behind him, the sharp slam of it enough to shatter whatever hold he had on her, startling her back to the world. On a deep huff, he walked around the back of the couch. She tracked him with her gaze as he crossed the worn floorboards to a twisting set of wooden stairs that led up into what she presumed was a loft bedroom.

"Are we leaving now?" She held her nerve when he stopped with his hand on the newel post and looked back at her, those glacial blue eyes giving nothing away.

"No." He mounted the first step.

No way was she going to let him leave it at that.

"When are we leaving? How far is it to the car?" She hobbled around the couch, choosing to head towards the cabin door, earning a glare from Rune as she neared it.

He could glare at her all he wanted. She wasn't his prisoner, not anymore anyway. She had the feeling that Saint was fine with her being here and that he wouldn't care if she walked out of that door, and she also had the feeling that Rune wouldn't be able to do anything about it. He didn't strike her as the sort who would go against the orders of the pride's leader.

"Soon, and we're not going by car." He turned away from her and managed to take another two steps before she stopped him in his tracks again.

"What do you mean, we're not going by car? Saint said you would drive me to the White Wolf pack." She frowned at him and gripped the cabinet to her right as her ankle throbbed.

"Change of plans," he grunted and again looked as if he wanted to leave it at that.

"So what is the plan now?" She wanted to growl when he still looked as if he wasn't going to elaborate. "I have a right to know. Maybe someone else at Black Ridge will be kind enough to tell me. Maybe they can take me to the White Wolf pack rather than you. There was that Maverick guy—"

Rune snarled.

Bone-chillingly, full-throttle snarled at her as if he was about to shift and rip her apart.

Callie locked up tight and blinked as she looked at him, as every instinct she possessed told her she had crossed a line somewhere, only she wasn't sure where. She held her ground when Rune stepped off the staircase, dropping to the floorboards with enough force to shake them, and her. He strode to her, not stopping until they were chest to chest, forcing her to tip her head back to keep her eyes locked on his.

Her wolf instincts wouldn't let her break his gaze, not this time.

This male was throwing off aggression, pulsing with anger, and he was a threat to her.

Wolves stared threats down.

"You're not going anywhere near Maverick." Rune glared down at her, his icy eyes filled with fury that she could sense in him too, rage that confused the hell out of her.

Was he angry because he viewed her as a potential threat to his friend, or was it because he didn't want that male near her?

"So you'll drive me?" She somehow managed to keep the wobble out of her voice, her words coming out strong and a little demanding.

He shook his head, his gaze never straying from hers. "No. I'm not taking you back towards the track. I won't lead the wolves on your tail back through the valley, risking not only my pride but the cougars too. We're getting as far from here as possible, in the direction you were already heading. There's a pass high up the mountain. We can cross into the next valley there."

Callie stared deep into his eyes, taking advantage of the fact his guard was down. She could see in them that he wasn't happy about being her escort, and she had noticed how his mood had shifted when she had mentioned Carrigan.

"Do you have a history with Carrigan I need to know about?" She let that question slip from her lips, braced herself because she was sure he would snarl at her again. She closely watched his eyes to chart the subtlest of shifts in his mood, just in case she needed to move out of his reach.

He bared fangs at her.

Pivoted away from her and stomped up the stairs, stripping his T-shirt off as he went, revealing heavily corded muscles that screamed of strength.

It was all the answer she needed.

Rune knew Carrigan. He knew Carrigan and she bet he knew exactly what kind of male the wolf was. There was a history there and that was the only reason he was willing to take her to the White Wolf pack, and the reason he didn't want her going off to find another guide and escort.

He wanted to meet the wolf who was after her.

She leaned against the cabinet beside her and gazed out of the window above it as she considered how to broach the subject of Carrigan with Rune. There had to be a way to discover his history with the male and whether she was walking into deeper trouble than she was already in.

Her ankle pulsed and ached as she dared to put her weight on it. She huffed and looked down at it. Grimaced when she saw how red and swollen it was. Trekking through the forest to reach Black Ridge had angered it, and now Rune was proposing she hike back to where she had been and walk even further than that.

Rune came back down the stairs, dressed in a fresh pair of black jeans and a matching long-sleeved T-shirt. In his right fist, he clutched another thick zip-up fleece like the one she was wearing. When he stopped and stared at her, she grew deeply aware of the fact his fleece was all she was wearing. She had half a mind to ask him to hurry and get those clothes for her, but a more pressing matter pushed to the fore, muscling it out of the way.

"I need to rest. My ankle is killing me. There's no way I can walk a long distance on it." She fully expected him to meet her request with gruff words and a demand that she do as he wanted.

For a heartbeat, he looked as if he wanted to say something, the usual ice in his eyes nowhere to be seen. They were soft, warm almost as they lowered to her right leg and he stared at her injury. That all changed when they shifted to the door behind her. His gaze turned glacial, losing all emotion.

The door opened and Callie swung to face it, keeping hold of the cabinet with her right hand so she didn't fall.

A tall, well-built male with wild blond hair and a thin layer of scruff coating his jaw, attempting to conceal the cute dimple in his chin, stepped into the room. A red-and-black plaid fleece shirt hugged his chest and arms, accentuating his muscles, and dark blue jeans that were worn in places clung to his powerful legs.

Hello handsome.

If she had been a feline, she might have purred.

Unlike her escort's, his blue eyes were warm and tropical, promised he was a more reasonable male than Rune could ever be.

He proved just how reasonable he was by holding the stack of folded clothes he clutched in his right hand out to her.

"I borrowed some clothes from my brother's mate for you. Hopefully they'll fit. I brought some bandages too. I've been learning about field dressing wounds and thought maybe I could help with your ankle." When he lifted his left hand, revealing a white plate stacked with bacon sandwiches, her mouth watered and she was torn between grabbing the clothes and grabbing breakfast. He shot her a sweet smile. "And these are from me. Saint mentioned you needed something to eat."

That was kind of him.

She had never seen such fluffy white bread or such perfectly cooked bacon, and the smell of them was incredible as a drop of butter eased down the crust to the plate. She almost moaned. Foodgasm. It was hard to resist the temptation to make grabby hands.

She tossed a pointed look at Rune, silently telling him he should be taking notes. Froze as a thought hit her.

"Is Rune your brother?" She looked at the blond, trying to spot a resemblance between them.

"Hell, no." The male leaned back slightly. He raised his hands when Rune huffed at his reaction. "Just… can't picture you as a brother. Suppose you and Maverick are like brothers."

She glanced back at Rune, caught the sour look on his face and the ice in his eyes that said this male was digging himself into an early grave and would be better off holding his tongue.

Rune stepped past her, grabbed the clothes and shoved them at her.

He swiped two of the bacon sandwiches from her bounty and growled, "Change. We leave as soon as you're ready."

She took hold of the clothes when he released them and tucked them to her chest as she scowled at him. "What about resting? I need to rest this ankle."

And for a moment, he had looked as if he was willing to give her the time she had asked for.

And then Mr Handsome had walked in and ruined everything, aggravating Rune just when he had been close to showing that soft side she knew existed beneath all the layers of razor-wire and reinforced steel.

"Change," Rune grunted, a sharp and cold edge to his eyes that said he wouldn't ask her again.

She got the hint, didn't need him seizing hold of her and marching her upstairs or anything like that.

"I'm guessing your mate didn't pick you because of your sparkling personality," she groused as she headed for the stairs.

Mr Handsome laughed. "Rune isn't mated."

Callie froze and looked back at him, her gaze clashing with Rune's wide eyes. They narrowed in an instant as he looked at the other male, as he hit him with a glare that made it painfully clear that he wanted to strike the male for putting that out there.

"I thought… You said there were unmated males here and I thought…" Her eyebrows rose as she recalled what he had said and she felt like an idiot. That old adage about assumptions hit her hard as she stared at him, unable to tear her gaze away. She had thought he was mated and now she felt like an ass. He had never said he was mated. He had only told her that there were unmated males at the pride. Apparently, that included himself. "You're not mated?"

She needed to hear him say it for some reason.

He shook his head and hit her with his patented glare. "Get dressed."

Callie obeyed that order, hobbled up the twisting staircase, but only because she needed a moment to think without him sucking the air out of the room, without being deeply aware of his presence. Rune wasn't mated. What on earth had made her assume that he was? Why had some deep, powerful part of her needed to hear him confirm he was unattached?

And why had that confirmation made her want to growl and close the distance between them?

She reached the bedroom, wanted to sink onto the end of the bed but hit a snag. The bed was nothing more than a double mattress on the floor, and not one that was thick enough for her to sit on without her having to struggle to get back onto her feet. Her eyebrows knitted as she ran over what she had seen of his cabin. It hit her that it looked more like a temporary shelter than any sort of permanent residence, as if he was ready to move on at a moment's notice and wouldn't have to leave anything of value behind when he did.

The more she came to know Rune, the less she understood him, and the stronger the feeling that there was darkness in his past grew.

Had that darkness involved Carrigan?

She gripped the railing of the stairs with one hand and set the clothes down on the bed with the other. She rifled through them and picked out a pair of black leggings that were thick, would be warm enough for the summer climate in the mountains but also a struggle to get off if she had to shift. They were better than nothing though. She grimaced and fought to get them on without falling and making a fool of herself.

"You going to be all right with doing this?" Mr Handsome said, concern ringing in his voice.

Rune grunted, "I'll be fine. I need to go speak with Maverick. Keep an eye on her, Lowe. Don't let her out of the cabin."

The door opened and closed again.

Callie was tempted to peek and see if she was alone with Lowe now, but focused on ditching her fleece and pulling on a worn, soft dark grey T-shirt that had a logo she didn't recognise emblazoned on the front of it. She covered that with a black fleece-lined hoodie and zipped it up. The fresh clothes made her feel a little better, but her thoughts weighed her down as the focus of them drifted beyond the sphere of her senses.

What was he going to talk to Maverick about? Her heart said it was about the black bear sow, Misty. The depth of the worry, and the love, Rune felt for that bear had surprised her, but it had also helped her see through a chink in his armour to the male he hid beyond it. Rune might growl and snarl, and roar, but underneath that tough exterior beat a warm heart.

At least it was warm towards those he cared about.

Like the bear.

Callie found herself praying the bears he had raised as his own cubs lived to reach thirty, just as he clearly hoped, because she had the feeling Rune had already lost too much and had been through enough pain in his life.

Gods, if he knew the course of her thoughts, he would probably bite her head off and turn moody and distant with her.

She hobbled back down the stairs and felt Mr Handsome's—Lowe's—gaze on her the moment she moved into view. He hurried over to her as she reached the bend in the staircase.

"Here, let me help." He held his hand out to her.

Callie placed hers into it. "Thanks. I didn't think I would find any gentlemen here."

Lowe chuckled. "You'll have to forgive Rune. He's a little rough around the edges, but he has his reasons."

Reasons she wanted to know.

"Here. Sit down and I'll bind that ankle." He jerked his head towards the couch.

Callie limped to it and sank onto the worn green cushions next to the plate of sandwiches and a stack of bandages. Lowe eased to his knees before her and carefully pushed the tight material of her leggings up her right leg.

"This is nasty." Lowe glanced up at her, looking like some kind of fairy tale prince about to slip a shoe on her foot and claim her as his princess.

Only she didn't want this shiny, perfect prince.

"A hunter's snare did it. I probably have tetanus." She forced a smile, trying to purge all thoughts about Rune and how different things would be if it were him kneeling before her, taking care of her.

She would have liked that a lot more.

She shook that thought away as she grabbed a bacon sandwich and stuffed half of it into her mouth. She frowned as she chewed, silently chastising herself. No, she wouldn't like Rune to swap places with Lowe, because he would be caustic and a terrible doctor, would probably hurt her or somehow use her injured leg as a means of threatening her into doing what he wanted.

"You know you can't get tetanus, right?" Lowe frowned at her, a wonderfully puzzled and concerned look in his sapphire eyes.

"It was a joke." She sighed and leaned back on the couch. "I'm too tired to make things sound like a joke. I haven't slept in a few days."

She popped the rest of the sandwich half into her mouth and reached for another, holding back a moan as her stomach growled for more.

"A few days?" Lowe opened a pack of cream bandages and applied the start of the roll to her ankle.

His hands were warm, his touch gentle, and his bedside manner was excellent. He would have made a good doctor. Females everywhere would have been hurting themselves just to get close to him.

"Guess you didn't get the memo that I'm on the run." This time, her smile was genuine.

The corners of his lips twitched but he kept his eyes on his work as he wrapped her ankle, the bandage tight enough that it hurt a little, but in a good way—as if it was holding her together.

"My mate was on the run when I met her." He glanced at her. "A little different to you though. Unless you have drug dealers on your tail?"

She shook her head and swallowed another bite of sandwich. She wanted to know more about his mate because she sounded interesting, but ended up staring at his nape as he bent forwards, trying to get a look at the back of her ankle.

She stared so hard at the point where the collar of his red-and-black fleece shirt met his spine that he stiffened and looked up at her.

"Sorry." She managed another smile. "Just trying to see if you had a tattoo too."

"Tattoo?" He sat back, his blond eyebrows furrowing as he pursed his lips.

"Like Rune has. I thought maybe you'd have a tattoo on the back of your neck too." She mentally cursed when she realised that she was close to rambling, was in danger of showing this male how nervous she was.

It wasn't the fact she was asking about Rune's ink that had her suddenly on edge though—it was the shift in Lowe's mood, one that didn't suit such a laidback male.

His blue eyes darkened rapidly, his lips flattening and the corners of them turning downwards as he frowned at her.

"You didn't bring up that number with Rune, did you?" His fangs flashed between his lips as he spoke, his gaze darkening further as she leaned back, away from him.

He must have seen the answer in her eyes, because he growled at her, rose sharply to his feet and stared down at her as brown fur swept over his hands and the corded muscles of his forearms to disappear under the rolled-up sleeves of his shirt.

She wanted to stand and distance herself, wanted to put the couch between them even when she knew it wouldn't stop him from getting to her if he wanted to attack her. She couldn't bring herself to move though, was caged within her body as she thought about that number she had seen, and how both Rune and Lowe had reacted fiercely to just the mention of it.

"What does it mean?" she whispered, cleared her throat and put some force behind her words as she gathered her courage. "Does it have something to do with Archangel?"

Before he could answer her, the door burst open and a male who looked just like Lowe, but with slightly darker and wilder hair, exploded into the room on a growl. Maybe she had been wrong about Lowe. This male was darkness, exuded danger in a way that made his twin look as easy-going as she had thought he was. Lowe's fury was nothing compared to the rage that burned in this one.

"What the fuck is happening here?" His dark blue eyes leaped from her to Lowe, and then back to her. He nudged his twin aside and loomed over her, flashing fangs at her and throwing off aggression that had fire flaring in her veins. "You got a problem with my brother then you've got a problem with me, Wolf."

"Knox." Lowe reached for the male's shoulder.

Knox growled at him before he could touch him, turned on her again and lunged for her.

Callie slapped his hand away before he could grab her, bared her own fangs and snarled, "Maybe that number means you're all some sort of genetic experiment. Did they want to create a race of asshole bears? If they did, they certainly succeeded!"

She gripped the arm of the couch and hopped up onto the seat, sprang over the back of it to land on the floorboards there, and regretted the hell out of it when lightning arced up her right leg.

"Number?" Knox slid a look at his brother.

"She asked Rune about his ink." Lowe didn't take his eyes off her, and the fact the darkness was leaving them wasn't a comfort to her.

Knox still looked ready to kill her.

"You know what? I'll find my own way to White Wolf Lodge. Honestly, risking being caught by Carrigan is better than dealing with any of you." She hobbled towards the door, her heart thundering, blood pumping so hard that her head hurt.

"Carrigan?" Lowe stepped into her path and she wanted to snarl and lash out at him to get him to move, but the warm look in his eyes, one of deep concern, had her holding herself back. "Carrigan is after you?"

She nodded and that bad feeling she'd had when she had mentioned that male to Saint and Rune returned, setting her on edge.

Lowe exchanged a look with Knox.

A grave one.

"If shit goes down, do *not* get in Rune's way or you'll be collateral damage." Knox's words shook her, had her wondering all over again about what had happened between Rune and Carrigan.

Lowe only made her bad feeling worse. "When the urge to fight comes over Rune, he loses himself to it. He can't help it. He won't mean to hurt you, but there's a high chance he will. He'll go right through you if it means getting to that bastard."

Before she could press the brothers for more than just that ominous information, Rune appeared in the open doorway of the cabin, his pale blue eyes colder than she had ever seen them as he glared at the twins.

For a moment, he looked as if he was going to demand to know what was happening, looked ready to lash out at Knox and Lowe, and maybe even her, but then he tossed a pair of boots at her.

Growled.

"Finish getting dressed. We're leaving."

Callie stared at him, a feeling rushing in her blood, chilling her.

Stopping the wolves on her tail from running into members of his pride or those from Cougar Creek wasn't the reason Rune was insisting they went to the White Wolf pack on foot.

The real reason was far less noble and far more dangerous.

Rune was using her as bait for Carrigan.

He had a score to settle with that male.

And Callie was going to find out what it was.

CHAPTER 10

Rune seethed as he trekked up the slope, following a narrow animal trail that was new, barely worn in. Callie's gaze landed on his back for the thousandth time, a brief caress that only made the silence between them more oppressive. She wanted him to shatter that silence, wanted to shatter it too if her heavy sighs were anything to go by, but neither of them knew what to say to each other.

Dark thoughts kept him quiet.

What was the cause of her silence?

He scented the air again, wanting to know if Carrigan was nearby, but only caught the soft fragrance of honeysuckle with a hint of caramel—a scent that had stamped itself on him the moment he had caught it and had realised it was coming from Callie.

A scent he was trying to purge from his memory and eradicate from his lungs, but it was impossible.

It seemed to have left an indelible mark on him, had quickly become a smell he would forever associate with the stubborn, angry wolf behind him.

And she was angry.

So was he, so they had that in common.

He wasn't sure whether it was the thought of crossing paths with Carrigan again that had him on edge, his mood constantly circling a dark abyss of rage that flooded him with a hunger to fight.

Or whether it had been the shouting match that had come from his cabin this morning, one that had seen him ditching Maverick and Misty and hurrying back to his home.

To intervene.

To protect the wolf.

Gods, in that moment rage had stolen control of him, swift to hijack his body as he had realised that not only Lowe was in the cabin with Callie—Knox had joined them. Knox who had a bad tendency to lash out first and assess the situation later. Sometimes the male was too much like Maverick. There was a fighter locked inside him, a beast that roared to the fore at the slightest provocation, had him itching to bloody his claws.

The thought that the male might paint those claws with Callie's blood had set Rune on the warpath, had clouded his mind with pleasing images of taking the male down, of putting him in his place and ensuring the younger bear knew not to mess with Callie again.

Knew the female was under Rune's protection.

The second Rune had realised what he was doing, had found himself standing in the doorway of his cabin about to launch at Knox and fight him, he had shut down the urge to rip him apart.

If only he could purge this restless, seething darkness that easily. His bear side paced constantly, only calmed whenever he made a mental note of how far they had come from the Ridge. That part of him liked the growing distance between him and the other bears—Knox and Maverick in particular.

He just wasn't sure why.

It had his mind going in circles, swift to skip over any explanation that involved Callie being away from Maverick and even Knox and Lowe.

"How long is it going to take to reach the White Wolf pack?" Callie's soft voice swept around him, calmed his bear side in a way that aggravated him and made him want to lash out at her.

He stoked his anger, keeping it at a simmer, using it as a shield to prevent her from seeing how easily she affected him.

It wasn't hard when he thought about the reason she wanted to reach the wolf pack.

He huffed. “Eager to get to Rourke?”

He felt her glare at his back, glanced at her as he reached a flat section of forest and the old track they had used before. She scowled at him, her amber eyes bright with irritation. Good. He didn’t want her getting comfortable around him.

Callie grabbed one of the saplings that was trying to grow along the track and used it to pull herself up the last few feet of the incline. She pressed her free hand into the short grass that had sprung up along the clearing and grunted as she managed to reach the track, bent over and breathed deeply. He was pushing her too hard. He glanced at her ankle, a flicker of concern running through him, vanquished in a heartbeat as he steeled himself.

She straightened and tipped her head up, her black hair falling away from her shoulders as she squared them. Looked him right in the eye. Bold. Brave. When she looked at him like that, silently challenging him, it roused a fierce need to growl and attempt to dominate her.

Rune shut it down, pivoted on his heel and started walking, heading north.

“Do you have a problem with everyone in this world or am I just special?” Callie bit out, making him want to look at her to see that spark of fire in her eyes.

A spark he liked far too much.

“You’re special all right,” he grunted and kept his eyes locked on the distant white peaks of the mountains. “I’m guessing you’re special to Carrigan. Is that why he’s hunting you? Did you have a lover’s spat and you walked out on him? Maybe that’s why you want to get to the White Wolf pack so badly… so you can shack up with another male. Trading up, Wolf?”

She was before him in an instant, her anger hitting him hard as she snarled in his face. “You know nothing about me and my situation, so lay off.”

Rune squared up to her, couldn’t help himself when her eyes were flashing fire and she was throwing off aggression, challenging him, rousing that inferno in his blood that he was beginning to like. "Enlighten me then. You're not Carrigan's lover?"

She growled.

"If I was, I'd be one of a whole bunch of them. The bastard has a harem at his pack." The fury, the fight, that had been in her words suddenly died and she rubbed her right arm as she glanced away from him, looking beyond him towards the start of the valley where the trailhead was. "I can't go back there. I *won't* go back there."

The desperate note her voice gained awakened something dark and fierce inside him, birthed a desire to fight Carrigan for her sake too. He wasn't a white knight, but he wanted to kill the wolf.

For her.

To set her free.

He stared at her, studying every subtle shift of her expression, every emotion that flitted across her eyes, his senses locked on her to detect even the faintest change in her mood. Hurt. Fear. Desperation. It was all there for him to read, none of it hidden from him. Whatever had happened to her at Carrigan's pack, it had shaken her. Had Carrigan been the one to abuse her?

"You said you were between packs. Was Carrigan's pack your original one?" He hadn't known how badly he needed to know the answer to that question, needed to know more about her, until it was out there, hanging in the air between them.

He willed her to answer him.

She shook her head. "No."

She wrapped her arms around herself, stiffened as she noticed what she was doing and dropped her arms to her sides. Rune got that. She didn't want to look weak in front of someone else. She didn't want to appear vulnerable.

Callie turned away from him and pulled her hood up, covering her raven hair. She jammed her hands into the pockets of her top as she walked, her limp still pronounced, following the track north towards the glacier and the pass.

Rune stared at her back, fighting the urge to ask her whether Carrigan had been the one who had touched her without her consent, scarring her deeply. He sighed, his shoulders heaving with it under his fleece, and went after her. He easily caught up to her but remained a few steps behind, keeping an eye on her, monitoring her mood with his senses, aware that she didn't need him pushing her right now.

Judging by the anger he could still feel in her, and the hurt, her mood was treading as dark a path as his was.

When they reached the end of the broad section of track, she glanced at him. He pointed towards a smaller path that branched off it, cutting across the thin grass and greenery to the trees that hugged the side of the mountain. She took it, her shoulders heaving in a sigh as she followed it up the steady, gentle incline.

She picked her way across a stream that washed part of the animal track away, tumbling down from the mountain towards a steep drop somewhere off to his left. There was a waterfall there, small but beautiful at times depending on how much rain they'd had, a place where he had often gone to sit for a time and be alone. The sun filtered through the trees into a pool at a certain time of day, making the water sparkle, and it was peaceful.

"My original pack was down near Revelstoke." Callie's voice broke into his reverie, drawing him back to her, and he held his tongue, aware she was fighting with herself, wanted to get the words out but was finding it difficult. If he talked, she would clam up again, and gods, some foolish part of him didn't want that. He wanted to know her story. Her shoulders shifted with her sigh—a sigh that wasn't melancholy. It reeked of hurt, tinged with betrayal. "Carrigan was doing business with my alpha and he expressed an interest in me. Edward handed me over as if I was his property and not a living being with my own free will."

"Son of a bitch," Rune growled, unable to hold his anger back as he looked at her, as he felt the hurt that had caused her and knew in his gut how betrayed she had to feel.

The thought of someone treating her like that had his bear side roaring to the fore, had him restless with a need to turn around and track Carrigan down to kill him, and then head to Revelstoke to deal with Edward. His blood burned with the urge to surrender to that need, to give himself over to it, had his fangs descending and pushed him dangerously close to shifting.

But then Callie stopped and looked over her shoulder at him.

Her bleak expression, the hurt and fear that shone in her amber eyes, stilled the turbulent emotions sweeping through him, had sudden calm washing through him instead as he stared into them.

The urge to hunt Carrigan down transformed into a powerful need to get Callie to the White Wolf pack as soon as possible, ensuring she was safe.

Made him realise what a monumental dick he had been, thinking only of how he felt, not even pausing to consider how she felt. Her desires, her fear and her desperate need to reach the safety of the White Wolf pack hadn't even factored in when he had made his decision to force her to trek to the next valley. He had thought only of what he had wanted, had viewed her as a path to getting the revenge and closure he needed.

Placing her at risk.

Rune growled and silently vowed that nothing would happen to her. They couldn't go back now. Getting back to Black Ridge for the keys to Maverick's truck and then getting to the trailhead would take too long and place even more people in danger. They had to keep going forwards. As much as he hated it, he had to trust that Rourke could keep her safe.

He looked ahead of her, to the point where the pass was. It was still a long way away, but they could make it. He could get her to the White Wolf pack before Carrigan found her. He could make things right.

As soon as she was safe, he would find Carrigan and deal with him.

The male would never bother her again.

Rune would make sure of it.

Made it an oath.

A promise he would keep even if he had to sacrifice his life to achieve it.

"Does Rourke know about this?" Rune closed ranks with her, his senses stretching around them as he fought the urge to press her to keep moving.

She needed a break.

She surprised him by shaking her head and continuing along the path, only to pause at another stream. She stooped and scooped up water, drank it and then looked at him.

"Why doesn't Rourke know about what happened to you?" He watched her, mesmerised by her graceful movements as she carefully scooped up another handful of water and sipped it.

She lifted her head. Shrugged.

"Why would he? I've never met him."

He frowned at that. "You don't know Rourke?"

Callie shook her head again. "No. I heard about his pack, about how he takes in wolves who no longer have a pack and takes care of them. I thought maybe he could protect me. He's my only way of getting rid of Carrigan. Rumour says he's helped other wolves like me."

Rourke the white knight.

Rune wanted to growl, leashed the urge but failed to shut down the sharp change in his mood judging by how Callie eyed him and looked ready to fight him again. He wasn't angry at her. Not really. He was angry at someone he had never really met, had only seen from a distance.

Irritated because she held the male in such high regard, talking about him as if he was some kind of wonderful saviour and the only one capable of helping her.

"I'm helping you, aren't I?" he bit out, unable to hold those words back, putting them out there in some needy and feeble attempt to make her think of him in the way she did with Rourke.

She scoffed and turned on her heel, giving him her back.

"You're using me as bait. I'm not an idiot, Rune. You have some unresolved business with Carrigan, and you're hoping he catches up with us so you can have your shot at him. What I don't understand is why you don't just wait here for the wolf and his men." She glanced over her shoulder at him, hitting him with a hard look that had him feeling like a dick all over again, and walked away from him. "Why bother pretending to take me to Rourke?"

That stung.

Had him taking fierce strides towards her, closing the distance between them down to nothing.

"I might be using you as bait, you're right about that, but I'm not planning to place you in danger. Waiting for the wolf here would do just that… especially if he has men with him like you say he does." Rune caught her arm, closed his fingers around it when she jerked it forwards, trying to break free of him, and spun her to face him. Her gaze clashed with his, the fire in it warning him he was treading on thin ice. He couldn't back down. The inferno in his blood raged too fiercely to be tamed, pushed him to make her see that she was wrong about him. "I'm leaving a scent trail for the bastard to follow, one that will lead him to the White Wolf pack, and hopefully it'll take him long enough to catch up with us that I'll have time to convince Rourke to team up with me to take Carrigan down."

Her eyes darted between his, her black eyebrows rising slightly as she searched them. "What if Carrigan catches up with us before then? Have you thought about what happens then?"

Rune growled, "I'll deal with him alone if that happens."

She laughed at that, ripping another snarl from him, this one born of the fact she was mocking him, truly thought he was incapable of protecting her.

"Really?" She squared up to him, her breasts dangerously close to pressing against his chest. "I can fight. You'll need me to fight too. The last time I saw him, Carrigan had ten of his best wolves with him."

Rune forced a huff from his lips, tried to ignore how close she was to him, how her heat warmed his thighs and chest, and her scent tormented him, flooded him with an urge that shook him.

He wanted to drop his lips to the smooth column of her throat and kiss it, ached to hear her moan in pleasure as she arched into him, seeking more.

What was it about this female that had him firing on all cylinders, willing to push aside his hatred of wolves to embrace the feelings she awoke in him, the needs she unleashed?

He stared down into her eyes, bewitched by the fire in them, by the strength that shone in them and the determination that tugged at a part of him, had him almost relenting because that part of him wanted to see her fight.

He bet she would be majestic.

Captivating.

He shut that side of him down. It wasn't going to happen. He had made a vow to protect her and he wouldn't fail, not this time.

But eleven wolves would be difficult to deal with alone.

He drew down a deep breath, denying the voice in the back of his mind that whispered at him, trying to convince him to let her fight. It wasn't going to happen. Just the thought of her in the thick of a fight against eleven male wolves had his fangs dropping and his bear side pushing for freedom, attempting to force a shift as his primal instincts roared at him to protect her.

If only the thought of her fighting unsettled him this much, the sight of her up against Carrigan and his men would send him into a rage so dark she might end up caught in the crossfire.

He couldn't bear that.

Rune stared at her, charting the sculpted planes of her face, the delicate blush of her lips, the gentle slope of her nose, ending with losing himself in the striking amber of her eyes. He couldn't let her fight. He wouldn't. He would protect her to the best of his abilities, would harness the side of himself that had been born in the cage, allowing no one to reach her.

He would keep her safe.

He had failed in a mission like this one before, what felt like a lifetime ago, but this time he would succeed. No one would touch Callie. No one would hurt her.

"You can't fight." He released her arm and walked past her, battling the rage that simmered in his veins, constantly pressing him to find something to fight in order to unleash the aggression building inside him.

"I can!" Callie snapped, stoking the heat in his veins back into an inferno.

Or maybe it wasn't rage that burned in his blood.

Maybe it was something far more dangerous.

Rune looked back at her, a wave of heat rolling over him, tightening his muscles and making him deeply aware of the beautiful, fierce female standing before him.

A female he had offended.

He shook his head.

"I didn't mean it like that, but I get why you think I did. How many males throughout your life have told you that you can't fight?" When he asked her that, the look she gave him said it had been a lot. Male wolves were overbearing, had a bad habit of holding females back and treating them like life was still as it was centuries ago. Bears knew better than to oppress their females like that. His breed had learned the hard way that you didn't tell a female what to do or try to hold them back. "I'm not one of those males, Callie. I know you can fight… but I'm not going to let you. I just can't."

She looked as if she wanted to make him explain himself.

"It isn't going to happen." He put force behind those words, needing to make himself clear, and saw it in her eyes the moment she realised why. He wanted to huff at that flicker of fear, wanted to growl and roar Lowe's name, sure it had been that male who had told her about him in his absence. He sighed instead. "Lowe told you to keep out of my way when I'm fighting, didn't he?"

Lowe had probably only wanted to protect her by giving her a head's up about Rune's temperament, but it still irritated him.

She shook her head, rubbed her arm and then let her hand drop to her side. "It was the other one. The asshole."

According to Callie, most of the bears in his pride were assholes. He figured she meant Knox. An image of how shaken she had looked when he had heard the ruckus in his cabin and returned to it flickered across his mind and the urge to fight Knox returned. Rune shoved it aside.

"Then you know that whatever goes down, you're not fighting. You're staying the hell away from it." He knew the moment he had royally screwed up with her, saw the darkness invade her eyes as her lips flattened and her scent gained an acrid note.

"You're just another overbearing male after all… thinking you can push me around and dictate what I do. Well, you don't own me and you certainly don't control me. You can't make me do anything," she bit out and strode past him.

Rune caught her arm again and twisted her to face him as he growled at her.

He meant to say something, wanted to defend himself and force her to agree to keep the hell away from the fight when it went down, only he was lost for words as her eyes met his. Anger shone in them. That fire he admired. She was a fighter. She was strong.

Stronger than Grace had ever been.

A flash of that delicate, pale-haired female overlaid onto Callie, and a need to tell her that he was sorry swept through him, together with all the rage and the grief that had consumed him in the months after he had failed her.

Rune reached his free hand up, aching to touch her face, to feel the warmth of her skin against his fingers again. He ached to hear her voice, to have her tell him that it wasn't his fault, that he hadn't failed her. He had fought as hard as he could, but it hadn't been good enough.

He hadn't been strong enough.

"Rune?" That soft voice wasn't the one he had wanted to hear, but it had warmth curling through him to melt the icy sludge in his veins, had light chasing back the darkness that had filled him, and pulled him back to the present.

To a beautiful wolf.

"What's wrong?" All the fire that had been in Callie's eyes was gone now, a softness replacing it that tore at him, threatening to rip down his strength and have him succumbing to the pain that blazed in his soul.

Rune turned away from her and ran a hand down his face. "I don't want to talk about it."

He walked for a few steps and then stopped and looked back at her.

"I can't let you fight. If I see you fighting, I'll lose my shit, and you'll be in even more danger."

He thought about Grace, locked in that cage, fighting for her life.

Thought about how powerless he had been to help her.

About how he had failed her.

He couldn't let that happen with Callie.

"Rune." Callie reached for him.

He pivoted on his heel. "Keep moving."

Rune tried to ignore the way she said his name, how it stirred something inside him whenever it fell from her lips, spoken so softly.

A warmth he hadn't felt in a long time.

No.

A warmth he had never felt before.

One that set him on edge.

One that felt dangerous.

He couldn't give in to it.

No matter how tempting it was.

CHAPTER 11

Callie's harsh pants were the only sound in the still world, seemed to echo through the sparse trees as she focused on following a faint track in the brown earth. She wasn't sure how Rune could see it, but then maybe he didn't need to be able to make it out among the old pine needles and fallen birch leaves in order to know where it was. He knew this valley, and knew it well judging by how easily he cut a path across the side of the mountain, gradually taking them higher and higher.

Either that or he was really good at pretending he knew where he was going.

She lifted her head and fixed her gaze on his broad back as he strode ahead of her at a clipped pace, one she hadn't failed to notice was steadily slowing as the hours wore on. She hadn't had a break since they had last spoken to each other and her feet were getting sore in her borrowed boots.

And the air between her and Rune was thick, heavy and choking.

Callie had been mulling over the way he had looked at her as if she was a ghost, how he had transformed before her eyes, going from a dark and dangerous brute who had been laying down the law with her to a soft, almost tender male who had looked as if he was lost.

Or maybe he had lost something.

She had the feeling there was a reason he didn't want her to fight, a reason why it would tip him over the edge, and her gut said it had to do with a female.

And that number inked on the back of his neck.

She stared at the spot where it was hidden behind the collar of his black fleece.

Thought about what Knox had told her and the things she had seen for herself.

Were Archangel the reason Rune had a darker side, one that was apparently violent?

Her boot scuffed the uneven ground when she failed to lift her foot high enough and she braced her hands in front of her as she tipped forwards, fearing she would fall on her face.

Rune's strong hand locked around her wrist, keeping her upright. As soon as she had her balance again and wasn't in danger of falling, he released her and carried on walking.

"I need to take a break." She leaned forwards and braced her hands against her thighs, and then rubbed the back of her right hand across her forehead, clearing the dampness away. She unzipped her hoodie slightly, enough that cool air washed over her chest through her grey T-shirt, bringing her temperature down.

Rune gave her a look that commanded her to keep moving.

Callie gave him a look that said it wasn't going to happen.

She limped to a nice thick trunk and sagged against it, exhaling hard as her aching body instantly felt a whole lot better.

The big bear huffed.

Stomped back to her.

He looked as if he wanted to bark an order at her, but then his expression shifted, losing some of the hardness, and he glanced at her leg.

"You can rest a short distance ahead. I know a nice spot." He looked over his shoulder and ran a hand over his close-cropped dark hair, an awkward gesture that made her believe he wasn't lying to her in order to get her to keep moving without kicking up a fuss.

She had figured out a few things about Rune, and this was one of them. He grew awkward whenever he did something nice for her, and shortly afterwards that war would erupt in his pale blue eyes—a battle between that softer side he was working damned hard to keep hidden and the side that growled at everything around him, treating the world as if everyone and everything in it was out to get him.

"Fine," she muttered and pushed away from the tree, already missing the support of it. She hobbled along behind Rune, trying to keep as much of her weight off her healing ankle as possible as she followed him up the incline. It was starting to feel better, wasn't giving her too much trouble, but she didn't want to press her luck.

The last thing she needed was Rune tossing her over his shoulder again because she was slowing him down.

Ahead of them, the trees began to thin. Callie squinted, peering beyond them. Was that a clearing? If it was, then it wasn't among trees. There was pure dark green beyond a patch of brighter green land, and she thought she could make out the sky.

Everything became clear as she neared it.

It was a sweeping curve of open land, a clearing that had grass on both sides of a worn track, and where the ground dropped away to her left and directly in front of her, there were shrubs and then the tops of trees. Mountains rose around her, snow dusting their peaks still, a sharp contrast to the sheer granite faces on some of them, and below those bands of grey were slopes of vivid green and then more dark treetops.

It was stunning.

Callie walked forwards, passing Rune, drawn to the edge of the clearing where the grass dropped away steeply towards the bushes and trees. She waved her hand in front of her face, wafting insects away, not wanting them to spoil this moment.

She turned to look at Rune as he grunted.

Held back her smile as he hefted a section of log and carried it over to her. He set it down and busied himself with dusting the dirt off his fleece and jeans, paying far too much attention to what he was doing.

If he was worried she was going to thank him, or maybe even swoon over his thoughtfulness, he didn't need to be. She knew him well enough now to know he would only growl and bare fangs at her, unable to accept her gratitude. She silently thanked him instead as she took a seat, sighed at how comfortable it was and how nice it felt to be sitting down, with the sun on her back and such a beautiful view spread before her.

She could stay here for hours. Days.

Might even go as far as building a cabin and living here.

She was sure she had never seen such an incredible view.

Rune stepped up beside her, closer to the edge, and stared out at the valley, his rough features etched in pensive lines as his blue eyes scoured the trees below them.

"What if Carrigan doesn't come after us?" She kept her eyes locked on Rune as he surveyed the valley. "Aren't you worried that he'll go to Black Ridge?"

He shrugged his broad shoulders and moved a step closer to her as he turned slightly, his sharp gaze scanning the valley to her left now. "Carrigan is following us. I'm confident of that."

"How can you be so sure?"

Rune slid her a look. "I have something the male wants."

Her lips flattened. She hated that. She hated that Carrigan wanted her. She hated that Edward had given her to him. She hated that she had been forced to leave her pack—her family—and that she could never see them again.

It was a weight around her neck, constantly dragging her down, and some days it was hard to find the strength to keep going. She had been on the run for weeks now, but she hadn't had time to stop and think about everything. Every second of her days and nights had been dedicated to keeping moving, to reaching the White Wolf pack. It was all she had thought about. Surviving. Staying ahead of Carrigan. Getting to Rourke.

Callie looked at Rune.

He had changed everything though.

For the first time since she had fled Carrigan's pack, she felt safe. That feeling of safety had her starting to think about things, and gods, she wished she could purge it all from her head and her heart.

"What's wrong? Your mood shifted." Rune spared her another glance, and then his aquamarine eyes drifted back to her and he lingered.

He had good senses.

Callie forced a smile and looked at the valley. "Just thinking about everything. These last few weeks have been the hardest of my life and I'm worried that everything I've done will be for nothing. I'm worried that all I've done is infuriate Carrigan by making him chase after me and that when he gets his hands on me, my life is going to be hell. I'm worried that Rourke won't give me protection… that he'll hand me back to Carrigan."

"None of that is going to happen, Callie." Rune moved another step closer to her, capturing the whole of her attention, sucking the air from her lungs as he gazed down at her, a touch of softness clashing with darkness in his eyes. "I'll get you to Rourke. Saint seems to think he's a good male and I'm sure he'll accept you into the pack. You'll be safe there."

She gazed up at Rune, felt deep in her heart that she was safe here too, with him.

That soft edge to his hard gaze made her feel he wanted to tell her that, but that he couldn't.

He wanted her to know she was safe with him.

He didn't need to say it for her to know, just as he didn't need to say it for her to know that if Rourke did reject her that she wouldn't end up in Carrigan's hands.

Rune would protect her in his stead.

She sighed, feeling a little awkward herself as she realised how much that comforted her, as the thought of Rune fighting for her freedom made her feel confident that her future was one where she would be in control of her own life.

"This valley is beautiful," she said, needing to fill the too-comfortable silence.

Rune smiled as he looked at it.

Gods.

It struck her that for all his darkness, for all his ferocity and his scars, and how cold his eyes could be at times, Rune was handsome.

Callie had been sure he didn't know how to smile, but there it was, and it was stunning, had her heart skipping a beat and her belly fluttering.

"It is beautiful," he breathed and then slid her another look. The banked heat in his gaze made her want to know what he was thinking and had a blush climbing her cheeks.

She averted her gaze. "How long have you lived here?"

"A little over twenty years, since Saint came to Vancouver and—" He fell silent again.

"And?" Callie risked a glance at him, found him glaring at his boots, his expression rapidly darkening as a wary edge entered his blue eyes.

She wanted to press him to tell her, but she knew it would be a mistake. Instead, she gave him space, time, just sat with him and waited it out, sure he would talk when he was ready.

Rune heaved a long sigh and pivoted to face the valley, his gaze locking onto a point off to her left. Black Ridge.

"This place is home." His deep voice held a warm note that told her how much he meant that, how deeply he felt that this valley and Black Ridge was the place where he belonged and where he wanted to be for the rest of his life. "The only one I remember. Around eighty years ago, hunters raided my pride. They took me and some others, and killed a whole lot more."

"Archangel," she murmured, her voice filled with the hatred she held for that hunter organisation.

Their apparently noble cause to protect humans from only dangerous non-humans, ones who threatened mortals, was a front that had many immortals fooled. Not her, and not Rune, judging by the anger she could sense in him. Shifter prides and packs all over Canada had been subjected to regular raids, weren't allowed to live in peace, even though they had done nothing wrong. None of them were a threat to humans. The hunters didn't care. They attacked at least one or two prides or packs a year, indiscriminately killing and capturing innocent shifters.

"What happened to you?" She resisted the urge to look at the back of his neck, her gaze drawn to the number there as if it was a magnet.

His expression lost all emotion. "They held us in a building. One used as a containment facility. Some of my kin were experimented on and studied, and the rest of us… we were the entertainment."

Her eyes widened as horror swept through her, a chill tumbling down her spine.

"Entertainment?" Sickness brewed inside her as she looked at the left side of his face, at the scar that darted over his temple and into his short hair, and had taken a nick out of his ear. She had the terrible feeling she knew what he meant by that.

Rune looked at her, a bleak edge to his blue eyes. "You're wary around me and I have the feeling Knox told you things he shouldn't have, so you don't have to pretend you don't know about the cage fighting."

Her mouth fell open. "Cage fighting?"

Rune cursed.

Callie shot to her feet. "Knox only told me not to get in the way if you had to fight. My gods… these hunters made you fight the other bears? Your own kin?"

He grunted. "Not just bears. Not just my kin. I've fought all kinds in my time."

Her eyes widened further as something hit her, chilling her blood. She was afraid to ask, wasn't sure she could bear to hear him confirm what she suspected, but she needed to know.

"You said you came here twenty years ago… and that you were taken from your pride almost eighty years ago. Rune… You're not telling me you were… Not for that long."

He shrugged. "No. Yes. I mean… I'm not good at talking about this… I'm not good at talking about anything, really. I've spent two decades struggling to adjust to this world, to functioning in society. It's all so alien to me."

He looked at the valley again, a lost edge to his expression, and her heart went out to him.

He had been a captive of Archangel for sixty years.

Had been forced to fight other shifters and gods knew what else for sixty years.

Good gods, it was little wonder he acted like this world was out to get him. It was little wonder that whenever he showed her that he was feeling softer emotions he reacted negatively, lashing out at her. He had probably spent those six decades hardening himself to protect himself, destroying any softer emotions that might be used against him or that might be viewed as a weakness by other shifters who fought in the cages, or those who had held him captive.

She had thought her life was bad, and it was, but it was nothing compared to what Rune had endured, to what he had somehow lived through and survived.

He heaved another long sigh.

"I fought in arenas for close to sixty years, but not the same ones. They moved us around. A few decades ago, they brought me to Vancouver. They'd set up a very professional outfit. Damned place looked like a nightclub. Two cages. One smaller one and then the large one where I fought." Rune shrugged, rolling his shoulders, but they remained stiff, his big body locked in a rigid pose and his eyes fixed on a single point in the distance. "They had at least thirty… maybe forty… shifters there at all times. Turnover was pretty high, but it didn't seem to bother the hunters. They replaced those who were killed almost immediately, like they had a damned farm somewhere just waiting to supply them with fresh stock for their cages."

"That's terrible."

Rune turned his head towards her and glared at her, as if her pity pissed him off, and she understood why he might feel that way. He was strong. A real fighter. He had survived decades of having to fight for his life, forced to kill in order to live to see another day.

"I'm sorry," she whispered, her gut churning with acid that scoured her insides as she caught a flicker of pain in his glacial eyes and knew it was only the tip of the iceberg. She could only imagine how much pain he carried beyond that wall of ice he had built around his heart. "I was nosy and I shouldn't have been."

Rune shrugged. "It's better you know. Now, when the fight comes, you'll know to stay the hell out of it and out of my way."

She knew that was what he wanted, that he was used to handling things alone, but she couldn't let that happen.

When the fight came, she intended to be in the thick of it, whether he liked it or not.

It was her life she was fighting for and he had to know how that felt. He had to know that she needed to take an active role in ensuring that the outcome of the coming fight was in her favour, and her future would be one where she was free.

But that wasn't the only reason she wanted to be a part of things.

Rune had fought so many battles alone.

She wanted to show him that it didn't have to be that way, that he didn't need to shun the help of others, or take on everything alone. She wanted him to see that there were people in this world willing to stand by his side and be there for him, to have his back and make sure nothing bad happened to him.

She wanted to protect him.

And she feared she knew why.

CHAPTER 12

Rune kept his focus on the trees that surrounded him, on the mountains that peeked through the green canopy from time to time, and on the flashes of blue sky. Anything to stop himself from shifting his senses to Callie. He didn't want to be aware of her, even when some part of him was—some deep, buried part of him where he wasn't quite master.

A part of him that had coaxed him into talking to her, into opening up a little to someone for once, all in some noble desire to show her that she wasn't alone and that he was more than capable of protecting her.

Only now he felt as if he had ripped open his ribcage and exposed his heart to her, and he didn't like it.

He stared at the trees. The mountains. The sky. Seeking calm in them, peace that eluded him as his mind constantly worked, churning as it ran over the things he had told her, as it broke down every reaction he had sensed and seen in Callie and studied it in detail, despite his best efforts to let it all roll off his back.

The feel of her eyes on his nape had him growling over his shoulder at her, warning her to stop looking at him. She scowled at him, a flicker of hurt in her eyes, and he cursed himself. He didn't mean to be angry with her, but he couldn't help it. Opening up to her had made him feel weak and the way she had looked at him, had spoken with that damned note of pity in her soft voice, had raised his hackles. Now he couldn't shake the urge to lash out at her, to blame her for everything, when she had done nothing wrong.

Rune scrubbed a hand down his face.

He was tired, moody about that too. He should have taken a moment to prepare before they had left Black Ridge. Instead, he had left home without any provisions or form of shelter, and the day was wearing on. Night at this time of year was still cold, hit figures low enough that sometimes it snowed up in the mountains. Sometimes it snowed a lot lower than the peaks too.

"How much further is it?" Callie grumbled.

Rune didn't want to tell her, because if he did, she was going to be mad at him.

He scanned the sky as he reached a point where the trees ended and the dirt became rock, charted the position of the sun and calculated how far they were from the White Wolf pack.

"A while," he muttered, because it was better than admitting it was still hours of hiking before they reached the wolves, and he had the feeling it would be dark before they made it there.

She sighed and he stopped and looked at her, a startling feeling rolling through him—concern. He took a good look at her, saw in the tight lines of her face that she was tired and her ankle was hurting, but she didn't mention it. She soldiered on, passing him and taking the lead.

It didn't make him feel any less of a dick.

"I could carry you for a while." Rune started after her.

She scoffed. "No thanks. My stomach is too empty again to have your shoulder jammed into it."

"I didn't mean—forget it." He stomped past her, told himself that she had every right to think he had intended to toss her over his shoulder since that was how he had treated her more than once before.

Callie stopped and stared at his back, a stunned edge to her voice as she said, "You were going to carry me nicely."

He huffed. "Offer's expired."

Her sigh said it all. Fine, he was being an asshole again, blaming things on her, not wanting to shoulder any of the fault himself. He didn't mean to be like that, but since he had talked to her, he had been slowly spiralling into the mother of all bad moods. He had only told Callie the bare minimum about his past, but he had been thinking about every little detail since then, couldn't stop himself from dredging up memories.

He glanced back at Callie, fear trickling through him as he braced himself. She had been looking at him differently since he had told her about the cages and his captivity, and he didn't like it. He didn't want his past to colour her opinion of him, didn't want her thinking he was some broken, messed-up male who had no hope of adjusting to this world.

Even when he felt as if he was.

She stopped prodding her ankle and lifted her head, her amber gaze softening as it landed on him, as she looked at his face. Clearly, he wasn't doing a great job of hiding how torn he felt around her, how on edge and off-balance she made him feel, because she looked as if she wanted to come to him.

She looked as if she wanted to wrap her arms around him, as if he needed her to hold him together.

He wasn't broken.

He wasn't.

Words rose to the tip of his tongue, but he denied them. He had already told her too much about himself, still couldn't believe he had confessed that he was no good at knowing how to behave around others. That had slipped from him before he could stop it.

But maybe it was good that she knew.

He cursed himself as he looked at her and thought about how he had treated her.

That secret part of him that wished he could be more like Saint, like Lowe, hell, even like Knox, pushed to the surface, making him feel even more inadequate and unequipped to deal with this world. Saint would know how to treat a female, even one from a breed he had no love for. Lowe would have been kind to her from the outset, helping her. Even Knox might have shown his good side to Callie rather than tying her up and questioning her as if she were a danger to everyone.

Callie slowly closed the distance between them, no trace of pity in her soft gaze, in the gentleness of her expression. He was grateful for that, hated how she had looked at him and didn't want her to think him any less of a male just because he had been through hell. She had been through her own version of hell, and while he felt bad for her, he would never treat her as if she were fragile and liable to break.

She was strong for surviving it and carrying on, for looking to the future and seeing something worth fighting for there.

She stopped close to him, her amber eyes bewitching him as the sunlight brightened them and caught the flecks of gold, bringing them out. Her rosy lips curled into the faintest of smiles as she angled her head back, causing her black hair to tumble away from her slender shoulders.

"Taking a break?" she said, her words as soft as her look.

He nodded.

Flexed his fingers at his side and resisted the urge that swept through him, a need so powerful that it was hard to deny it.

He wanted to tunnel his fingers into her glossy onyx waves and tug her to him, until she was pressed against him, her soft warmth heating his body.

He wanted to kiss her.

Instead, he stared down at her, his mind rolling back years to attempt to recall the male he had been before the cage. Had he been a good male, like Saint and Lowe? Good but a little wild, like Knox? Had he been a male who would have been worthy of someone as beautiful as the wolf standing before him?

His memories of the male he had been before the cage were too dim though, like faint shadows that slipped through his fingers and turned to smoke whenever he tried to grasp them.

He knew one thing though.

Whoever he had been, he wasn't that male anymore.

What did Callie make of the male standing before her?

He wanted to know, but at the same time he feared hearing what she thought of him. He hadn't been kind to her. There was a high chance she hated him and he deserved that.

Yet she was comfortable around him, and the way she looked at him at times made him feel that she trusted him.

He wasn't sure what he had done to deserve that trust.

For a heartbeat, she looked as if she might say something, but then she looked away from him, gazed out at the valley and sighed.

Rune looked there too as he thought about his pride and about her reason for wanting to get to Rourke. They were both the same in a way. Both of them had lost something important to them and both of them had been forced into a cage, taken against their will, and both of them had ended up needing to find a new home.

"Thinking about home?" Callie murmured.

He glanced at her, a flicker of a frown knitting his eyebrows as he cast her a look that he knew had conveyed his confusion since she smiled.

"You have that look I think I wear when I'm thinking about home." Her shoulders lifted slightly and then dropped as she sighed, as her eyes roamed over the mountains and the trees, a faraway look in them.

Had her home been as remote and wild as this valley? Anywhere near as beautiful? He passed through Revelstoke every time he and Maverick drove to Vancouver for the winter, escaping the snow and the urge to hibernate that had started coming back to him in the last few years.

He made a mental note to stop in Revelstoke the next time he had cause to be passing through and check it out. He wanted to see where Callie had grown up. He wanted to see the place she had called home.

"I was." He stared in the direction of Black Ridge, torn between telling her what was on his mind and keeping it to himself. Telling her won. "I don't remember where I grew up. I don't remember anything about the time that came before—well… It doesn't matter anyway. This is home now."

"I hope I can find a new home in the White Wolf pack." Those words were quiet as they slipped from her lips, had his gaze gravitating to her again.

He was sure that she would, and he was sure she would feel as moved by the acceptance into a new pack as Rune had felt when Saint had offered him a place in his pride.

Rune had felt humbled and unable to believe Maverick when the male had tried to convince him that Saint wanted to accept them into his pride.

He had been convinced the grizzly would turn them away. Hell, he had been convinced that Maverick would leave him and he would end up alone.

Instead, he had ended up with a new family and a place where he felt he belonged, somewhere he could heal and become a better male, and he counted his blessings every damned day.

"You'll find your home," Rune said, sure of that, feeling it in every beat of his heart as he gazed at Callie. A spark of hope lit her eyes and he found he liked seeing it, and liked that he had caused it. "The White Wolf pack will be good to you, Callie. They'll be like Black Ridge is for me—a new family."

He averted his gaze when she looked across at him, stared into the distance at the mountains and the forest, at the glittering snake of the creek as it wound its way down from the glacier, peeking through the canopy of rich deep green in places.

Rune flexed his fingers and curled them into fists.

Exhaled.

"I'm sorry about how I was with you." He let those words slip from him, didn't think about them, just let them spill from his lips. If he thought about them, he would feel that stab of vulnerability again and would fight them, would probably end up lashing out at her, blaming her for the fact he had opened up a little, when in reality he wanted to let her in. He wanted her to know him better. Gods help him. Gods help her too. He huffed. "Black Ridge… Saint and Maverick… Lowe and Knox… all the females… they're my family and… I'd do anything to keep them safe. I'd die for them if it came down to it. My history with wolves is not great, and I'm trying to overcome it, but it's hard sometimes. When I smelled Carrigan on you, I didn't know it was his scent until you mentioned him and it all made sense. I smelled him on you and I got angry… and I'm sorry."

There.

It was all out there now.

She could either forgive him or damn him.

It was out of his hands.

"Carrigan is the reason you hate wolves," she whispered.

Rune nodded and swallowed hard, braced himself against the images he knew would play out in his head like some twisted horror movie, or a nightmare where he had no control over the outcome of events.

But Callie placed her hand on his arm, and instead of being bombarded by images of Grace having to fight a huge polar bear male, all his focus was drawn to her. He stared at her, aware of how lost and wounded he looked, aware that all the pain he still carried in his heart, all the shame, was there in his eyes for her to see.

"I won't ask," she murmured, three words that offered him relief, together with that look in her eyes that told him that if he ever wanted to talk about what had happened in his past, no matter what it was, that she would listen.

And she wouldn't judge him.

The part of him that constantly expected her to turn her back on him, that constantly expected everyone to do that, faded into the background as he gazed down into her eyes, losing himself in them.

Warmed by the fact she hadn't distanced herself now that she knew a little about his past and the sort of male he was.

If anything, she had moved closer to him instead.

"We should probably get moving." She smiled, an awkward edge to it as her hand dropped from his arm, grazing his elbow, and she hobbled away from him.

Rune followed her, that warmth she ignited in him spreading as she dropped back to walk beside him as the track opened up, snaking around the side of the mountain. It wasn't far to the pass now. Maybe they could make it to the White Wolf pack before dark.

He glanced at Callie, a sudden need to stop that from happening striking him. He needed more time with her, found himself thinking of a thousand ways to delay her reaching Rourke and leaving his side. He had only just met her, but she had left her mark on him, had utterly bewitched him in less than a day.

And he had the feeling that if he had more time with her, she would do more than that.

She would make him fall for her.

That scared him a little, had him wanting to draw away from her and bring up barriers between them even as a part of him wanted to move closer to her instead, craved being near her and was eager to discover what would happen if he didn't push her away.

They trekked in silence, every minute feeling like an hour as he wrestled with himself, as he tried to be on alert and failed dismally. Callie didn't share his problem. Her focus was seemingly on the world around them at all times and he couldn't get his away from her. Maybe he was reading into things, seeing what he wanted to see whenever she dared to glance at him, whenever they had been close to each other over the past day.

There had been a spark of interest in her eyes more than once. Had he imagined that or was she attracted to him?

He glanced at the scant distance between them, watching her hand swaying back and forth so temptingly close to his. If he moved his hand only a few inches towards her, he could easily brush her fingers. How would she react to that?

Would she draw away? Be horrified? Or would she give him that look she had a few hours ago, when he swore she had wanted him to kiss her?

Rune battled with himself over the next mile, fighting the urge to touch her hand so he could know whether he was alone in his feelings or not.

"Is this the pass?" Callie looked at him, her gaze searing him, setting his blood on fire.

He lifted his eyes from her hand, locking them on her face. Evening light cast a glow over her delicate features and darkened her hair, and his breath hitched as her wide luminous eyes met his. Gods, she was beautiful.

When a puzzled look knitted her fine eyebrows, he cleared his throat and shook himself out of his reverie.

"Yeah," he grunted. "Still a few miles to the other side though. We'll follow the river."

"River?" Her eyes gained a curious edge.

He nodded. "Cuts through a ravine not far from here. Comes off the glacier. There's a nice waterfall around halfway along the pass where the trail drops towards the White Wolf valley."

And Rune wanted to stop there, wanted to sit with Callie a while and see if she found it as beautiful as he did.

"Let's go then." She smiled at him again, hitting him hard in the heart with it.

He could only nod as he tried to gather his wits, attempting to shake off the debilitating effect of that smile. She made him weak in a way no one had before her. Not even Grace. Something about this wolf stripped him of his strength and had him willing to fall to his knees before her if she would only gift him another glorious smile.

Hell, he would settle for just the chance to look into her eyes.

Gods, he was done for.

He had seen enough bear males at Black Ridge mooning after their females to know that he had it bad for Callie and that leaving her at the White Wolf pack was going to be hard. Maybe it was for the best though. A bear like him didn't deserve a female like her. He didn't deserve any female.

Rune dropped his gaze to her hand again, the urge to brush her fingers with his growing stronger by the second.

What if he risked it all and she rejected him?

It was only a few miles to the wolves now and he could leave as soon as he had dropped her off. He hadn't known her long and she probably wouldn't bust his heart, and he would get over her, resuming his normal life.

What if he didn't risk it all?

He would never know her true feelings, would drop her off at the wolves and return to Black Ridge, and probably end up plagued by thoughts of her and what might have happened.

He frowned at her hand.

What if he risked it all and she accepted him?

He would be the luckiest damned bear on Earth.

Having Callie by his side, in his life, filling it with warmth and light would make even the hardest days easy to face. He was sure she could heal him, maybe even restore him to be a semblance of the male he had been before the cage, and he would be blessed to have her.

Rune went in circles, debating which path to take. Risk it or don't?

They turned a bend in the track, a point where it narrowed and forced Callie to move closer to him. He stared at her hand. There were less than two inches between them now. It would be so easy to graze her fingers with his, and if she reacted badly, he could play it off as an accident.

Rune swallowed his racing heart.

Made a decision.

Risk it.

He eased his hand towards hers.

Callie tensed and pivoted to face the way they had come.

Rune didn't need to ask her what was wrong as a breeze swept around the mountain to gently blow her hair from her face.

He smelled wolves.

CHAPTER 13

Rune's senses sharpened, stretching around him to chart everything in the vicinity. He growled when he picked up the wolves' signatures. Callie hadn't been lying. Carrigan had ten men with him.

He didn't like those odds.

Rune seized Callie's hand and tugged her with him as he broke into a run. She stumbled as she twisted to face him, as she struggled to catch up with him. His heart thundered, blood pumping hot and hard as he kept his focus locked on the path behind him. If they were lucky, he and Callie could reach the crossing before the wolves caught up with them and they would be safe for a while.

The urge to fight Carrigan was strong, but his need to protect Callie was stronger.

The thought of her ending up captured by Carrigan and his men drove him, had him running harder, desperate to outpace the wolves who were moving swiftly behind him. They must have sensed him and Callie and started running the second they had. Fuck.

Rune cast a glance over his shoulder.

His heart jolted into his throat as he spotted the wolves. Several of the males were big, rivalling his size. Not good. His gaze locked with Carrigan's and an urge to turn back and attack the male swept through him, the need to avenge Grace strong and almost overwhelming him.

Callie's gasp as she looked back too was enough to shove that urge out of his head.

He couldn't fail her.

Wouldn't.

He needed to get her to safety, would uphold his vow to protect her. Nothing would happen to her. He looked at her. Saw a flash of blood-soaked skin. Shook it off. Memories roared up on him despite his efforts to deny them, tore at his strength as images from that night flickered through his mind, as Grace's harrowing screams chilled his blood.

"Rune!" Callie barked.

He snapped back to her, the darkness of his past falling away as he sensed what had her panicking.

Two of the wolves were closing in fast.

"Stop them!" Carrigan roared.

Rune looked back and growled as he saw two of the males had shifted, were running at them in their animal forms now—one a sleek grey wolf and the other a dusky brown.

Instinct took over.

Rune grabbed Callie, hefting her over his shoulder as he ran harder, silently apologising to her as she bounced on his shoulder, grunting every time her stomach came down on it.

"I can run by myself!" She sounded as angry and offended as he had figured she would be, but she made no move to get out of his grip. She clung to him, fiercely holding on to his black fleece, and her heartbeat was off the scale, drumming frantically in his ear. "Oh gods. Look at that drop."

Rune was trying not to look at the deep ravine just feet to his left. He was trying not to think about how the rock fell away into nothing or how one wrong step could send both him and Callie plummeting to their deaths.

The scent of her fear drove him, making him push past his limit as he spotted the bridge ahead of them.

If he could reach it, he could fend off the wolves and give her a chance to get to safety.

His senses blared a warning that he wasn't going to make it.

The wolves were too fast.

Rune dropped Callie close to forty feet from the crossing and shoved her towards it. "Run for the bridge."

He turned and bared fangs at the two large wolves, readying himself as they hurtled towards him, malice in their sharp eyes together with a hunger he was familiar with. They wanted to fight. He would give them one.

"What bridge?" Callie hadn't moved and he wanted to growl at her for that, wanted to snap that she wasn't helping him keep his head by lingering. He knew when she had spotted the crossing because she yelled, "That is *not* a bridge!"

"Get your damned backside across it." He reached around behind him and shoved her towards it, backed up with her as the wolves closed in.

Callie left his grasp and he sensed her moving away from him, turned his focus back to the wolves and tried to reassure himself that she was going to be fine. He would make sure of it. She would get across the bridge and she would be safe.

No one was going to hurt her.

The need to protect her that had been growing inside him since he had met her transformed into a powerful primal urge as he faced off against the two wolves, as awareness of the other nine that were closing in drummed in his veins.

"I can't do this." Callie's voice shook and he growled as he sensed her fear.

"You can. I need you to cross that bridge, Callie. Please?" Because if she didn't, he was going to lose it, and he wasn't sure she wouldn't end up caught in the crossfire. He didn't want to hurt her. Just the thought of it sickened him, made him feel wretched.

"Okay. I'll try." She shuffled a few steps forwards.

He wanted to shout at her not to 'try'. He needed her to do it.

The grey wolf put in a burst of speed and leaped at Rune, sailing through the air towards him. Big mistake. Rune was ready for him, grabbed him as he barrelled into him and twisted his body, flinging him to his right.

Over the edge of the deep ravine.

The male shifted back and screamed as he plummeted towards the river far below.

Out of the corner of his eye, Callie gasped and flinched away, locking up tight at the very start of the bridge.

"Go!" Rune barked.

She tensed and wobbled, shrieked as she desperately clung to the old ropes that formed the handrails of the ancient wooden footbridge.

Rune grunted as the brown wolf smashed into him, bellowed as the bastard sank his fangs into his left arm, ripping into his flesh in the same spot Callie had less than a day ago. He wrestled with the wolf, smashed him repeatedly in the top of his head with his right fist. When Rune grabbed his ear and yanked, almost ripping it off, the wolf yelped and released him. Rune bared his fangs as his arm throbbed, sickening waves of heat rolling up it, and locked his senses back on Callie for a heartbeat, needing to know she was safe.

His eyes widened as she shot past him, a blur of black fur. She snarled as she leaped on the dusky wolf's back, vicious as she sank her fangs into the male's nape and shook him. The male wolf growled and snapped fangs at her, twisted and tried to get hold of her. She released him and leaped back, bared bloodied fangs and looked ready to attack him again.

Rune grabbed her by her nape as she lunged forwards, stopping her and earning himself a black snarl. He kicked at the brown wolf as the male launched at her, knocking him away and sending him tumbling towards the ravine. His hindquarters went over the edge and he scrabbled with his front paws, whining and desperately seeking purchase to stop himself from falling as he shifted back.

Rune bundled Callie under his arm, ignoring her snarls and growls, because he wasn't going to release her and let her get herself killed. He grabbed her clothes as he passed them at the start of the bridge, aware she was going to want them once she had cooled off enough to shift back. The second he stepped onto the worn, sun-bleached wooden boards of the bridge, Callie went deathly still. Apparently, even in her wolf form she was afraid of it. It worked for him, allowing him to move without fear of dropping her.

He kept his focus locked behind him as he carefully placed each foot, testing the board to see if it would take his and Callie's weight before committing to standing on it. The narrow bridge swayed and creaked with each step he took and his mouth dried out, his muscles aching with the tension as he moved further along it, passing the middle. Just twenty, maybe thirty feet to go. They could make it.

The brown wolf reached the start of the bridge behind him and in the distance someone howled. Callie stiffened and then growled, twisting and turning in Rune's arms, trying to break free of his hold.

He tightened his grip on her. "Shh, Callie. Bastard isn't going to reach you."

Judging by her reaction, it had been Carrigan who had howled, no doubt to command the rest of his wolves to follow the one that was hot on Rune's heels now.

Rune risked it as he sensed the male closing in on him, mentally crossed himself and prayed to his ancestors that the old, fraying bridge could take it and he wasn't about to get him and Callie killed.

He ran.

The wooden boards groaned beneath his weight with each heavy step as he raced for the other side of the ravine, his eyes fixed on it, his senses guiding him. Behind him, the wolf snarled and put on a burst of speed. Rune clutched Callie to his chest as one of the boards gave out beneath his right boot, his heart shooting into his mouth and staying there even as he left the gaping hole in the bridge behind and closed in on the two thick wooden posts that marked the end of it.

He didn't feel any sense of relief as he hit the other side of the ravine, didn't even pause for breath. He hurled Callie clear of the bridge and turned back towards it, shoved and kicked at the nearest post until it wobbled.

Rune bent and grabbed it, wrapped his arms around it and heaved upwards, every muscle in his body straining and burning as he wrenched the post free of the rock and earth. A grunt burst from his lips the second it was free and the weight of the bridge yanked him forwards, towards the edge of the ravine. He quickly released the tall wooden post and glanced at the bridge.

The brown wolf had shifted back again, desperately clung to the remaining rope railing, his bare feet pressing to the ends of the wooden boards that now dangled vertically below him. The male's dark eyes widened as Rune moved to the other post and he frantically shook his head as he began moving, quickly edging along the tips of the boards.

Rune showed him the same courtesy he had given every male he had fought in the past, every one who had fallen to him in the cage and outside it.

He looked him in the eye as he grabbed the frayed top rope attached to the remaining post and broke it in two. The male dropped as the rope lost tension, scrabbled and grabbed hold of the wooden boards, clinging to them.

Rune broke the remaining rope.

The wolf screamed as the bridge dropped, desperately twisted and managed to get his fingers between two of the boards, his bare body plastered to the rest of them as the bridge swung towards the other side of the ravine.

Bastard might live to see another day.

Rune winced as the bridge hit the rough rock wall of the ravine and bounced the male loose, hurling him into thin air.

Or not.

The wolf plummeted into the rushing water and was lost beneath the turbulent white surface.

Rune lifted his head and stared across the fifty-foot gap to the nine males standing on the other side, the whole of his attention locked on one of them.

Carrigan stood just in front of his men, the hems of his black fatigues fluttering in the wind that tousled his blond hair, tugging shoulder-length strands loose from the knot he had tied it back in. He breathed hard, his dark green jacket tightening across the breadth of his chest with each one, and took a step forwards, narrowing the distance between them down to as little as possible.

Rune stepped up to the edge of the ravine and stared him down, locked in a silent battle with him. Even at this distance, he could sense the rage in Carrigan, could see the shock the male was trying to hide as he glared across the gap at him. Rune grinned at him, satisfaction rolling through him.

Surprise.

He wanted to holler that word, but settled for continuing to stare at Carrigan in silence, savouring the male's shock, how his face slowly darkened and the anger Rune could feel in him grew stronger. A male who didn't know him as well might think that Carrigan would give up his chase now he knew Callie had an escort—a protector—but Rune knew him. Carrigan wasn't happy that their paths had crossed and that he was protecting Callie, but it wouldn't stop him from coming after her.

The male always had been a cocksure bastard.

Back at the compound, that part of his personality had seen him rise in the esteem of the hunters and had gained him their protection and countless benefits as he had betrayed his own kind, snitching to his masters about the smallest things to please them.

This time, it would be his downfall.

Callie trotted up beside him.

Glared across the ravine at Carrigan, her amber eyes bright with a hunger for violence.

Rune reached out to brush his hand over her black fur to soothe her.

Callie broke away from him and ran.

CHAPTER 14

Instinct pushed Callie to run. Instinct to escape Carrigan and a life in slavery. Instinct to draw Rune away from danger. The moment he moved to pursue her, she ran harder, luring him into the forest that lined the sloping side of the mountain.

"Callie." Rune's deep voice rolled over her, soothed her fear even as the scent of his blood stoked it. "You're safe now. Slow down!"

She couldn't.

She wasn't strong enough to fight the primal urges that had stolen control of her, could only obey them. Wind played in her fur, cold against her face as she thundered through the evergreens, leaping bushes and kicking up pine needles. She savoured it as it filled her lungs, cooling her blood, helping her slowly claw back control together with the growing distance between her and Carrigan.

Ahead of her, a stream crossed a clearing, glittering like a river of diamonds nestled among green velvet in the sunlight.

"Callie," Rune called.

She skidded to a halt near the narrow stream, ending side-on to him, and looked back at him as sunlight bathed her fur, warmed it and soothed her further.

The moment her eyes landed on Rune, the instinct to run disappeared. He tucked her clothes beneath his right arm and huffed as he placed his hand over his left forearm, over the darker patch on the sleeve of his fleece.

The instincts screamed at her again, demanding she go to him. Her male was injured. She obeyed them, trotting to him as he entered the clearing. When she reached him, she tilted her head up and nuzzled his arm, licked it as the urge to clean it and tend to him stole control of her.

His pale blue eyes raked over her, concern shining in them as he settled them on her right hind leg. She looked there and bent her head around, lapped at the blood trickling down to her paw.

"You hurt yourself. Let me take a look." Rune eased to his knees beside her.

Calm suffused every inch of her as he ran his palm along her side, over her hips, and down her leg. Heat followed it as he leaned towards her, as his rich, earthy scent swirled around her, triggering a fierce reaction in her, one that swept through her and was too powerful for her to hold back.

Callie shifted back, framed his face and kissed him.

The primal instincts that had been dictating her actions faded now that she was in her human form and she froze with her lips pressed to his, shock rolling through her as she realised what she had done.

And how fiercely her body ached.

Every millimetre of her skin felt too sensitive, the slightest breeze making her shiver and sending subtle thrills through her, and inside she felt as if someone had cranked her tight, as if she needed someone to break a chain or kick open a floodgate to let all the tension explode from her.

And gods she needed that someone to be Rune.

He eased back slightly and cleared his throat.

Callie remained where she was, frozen like a statue as she replayed what had just happened. Not the kiss. What had come before it. She couldn't believe how she had reacted when she had seen Rune fighting, how desperately she had needed to protect him when that wolf had hurt him.

She hadn't been able to stop herself from shifting and leaping into the fray.

Silence stretched between them, thick and heavy, pressing down on her, and she struggled to find something to say, needing to shatter it.

"How… how long will it take Carrigan to get around that ravine? Are we even on the right side of it?" Her words came out shaky, betraying her nerves, but Rune didn't pick her up on it.

He was too busy staring at the narrow strip of grass between them, diligently keeping his eyes off her bare curves.

Gods, she felt like a fool. A blush scalded her cheeks and she wanted to beg him to forget what she had just done, to pretend it had never happened, even as she wanted to kiss him again.

Wanted to take it further than that.

Her body was on fire for this male, the flames refusing to abate as the seconds ticked by. In fact, she feared they were growing stronger, on the verge of transforming into an inferno that might consume her if she didn't do something to quench them. She had never felt like this, had never been this needy, and she feared her suspicions about Rune were right.

There was one way to find out.

She shook that thought away.

Rune hadn't kissed her back.

That was a huge red flag, one she would be a fool not to take heed of.

"The ravine is caused by the river that branches off from the creek that runs through Black Ridge. It flows all the way to the White Wolf pack territory. Carrigan can't get across it for a few miles, but if he follows it, it will lead him there." Rune's voice sounded as tight as she felt inside, his words gruff and low-spoken, husky almost.

She risked a glance at him, shivered when she found him gazing at her breasts before he shifted his gaze off to his right.

Did he want her?

If he did, he would have kissed her. Surely?

His blue eyes lifted to meet hers, lingered as an uneasy silence settled over the glade again.

There was banked heat in them, a look that made her feel he did want her, but he was fighting it for some reason.

Callie planted her right hand against the short grass near his thigh and leaned towards him, her gaze holding his as she murmured, "What are you thinking while you're looking at me like that?"

Rune startled her by seizing her nape with his left hand.

Swallowed her shocked gasp in a hard kiss.

Callie groaned and leaned into him, pressed her hands to his shoulders and pushed him back onto the grass as the hunger riding her got the better of her. The ache worsened with each fierce brush of his lips across hers. A thrill chased through her, stoking the fire to an inferno as he angled his head and deepened the kiss, his tongue demanding entrance. Callie opened for him on a trembling moan, shivered as his fingers tightened against her nape, holding her immobile as he devastated her with his kiss.

Her fingers found the start of the zipper on his fleece and she yanked it open, the rasping sound loud in the glade, causing another thrill to bolt through her. Rune groaned as she planted her hands to his chest, feeling the heat and hardness of him through his black T-shirt. It wasn't enough.

She growled and grabbed the hem of the garment, shoved it up to reveal bare skin, and groaned and shuddered as her skin made contact with his. Wicked urges hijacked control of her, the need he had triggered in her rising back to the fore to overwhelm her. On a vicious snarl, she peeled her mouth away from his and drank her fill of his body, her need to see it too powerful to deny.

A shiver wracked her.

Fire ravaged her.

Gods.

Rune breathed hard, his T-shirt askew, revealing the muscles of his torso as they strained with each rise and fall of his chest. His gaze seared her and she could almost feel him waiting to see what she would do.

Callie was torn between kissing and licking every delectable inch of him, and stripping him bare and riding him into oblivion, until this hunger was sated.

Rune made her decision easier for her by grabbing her right arm and pulling her back to him. He claimed her lips in another bruising kiss, dropped his hand to the small of her back and pinned her to him as he drove her wild. A shudder rolled through her as he brushed the fingers of his other hand across her left breast and cupped it, palmed it in a maddening way.

Too much.

On a low growl, she mounted his thighs, wrenching her body away from his touch. He groaned as she attacked the button of his black jeans, moved his hands there and helped her, his actions jerky and hurried, as frantic as she felt inside. She needed him. Felt as if she might explode if she didn't hurry.

Rune undid another button on his fly and some part of Callie decided it would have to be enough. She gripped his jeans and yanked them down his hips as she eased back, moaned as her gaze fell to the rigid steel of his cock. Oh gods. The need only grew worse, more desperate, making her wild as her mind raced ahead to imagine him inside her.

She wanted to stroke him, to touch and explore him, but there wasn't time. She gripped his hard length, relished his rumbling moan of pleasure as she fisted it, and vowed that next time they would do things slower, would indulge her need to chart every inch of his incredible body.

Callie raised herself off him on her knees and leaned forwards, planted her left hand to the broad slabs of his chest as she guided him into her. He growled as she sank back onto him in one swift downward plunge of her hips, his hands shooting to her waist to grip it hard. Fire ignited in his eyes as she wriggled on him, savouring the way he filled her, how well he fitted her.

As if they were made for each other.

That feeling that they were came over her again as she began riding him and he moved in time with her, lifting her up and filling her on her downwards stroke. She stared down into eyes that were no longer cold or filled with ice. They were burning, searing her as he kept them locked on hers, as he drove into her, his pace quickening. She moaned with each thrust of his length into her that sent sparks skittering through her, cranked her temperature up another degree and had her leaning forwards, her actions growing more desperate as she spiralled towards release.

Rune gritted his teeth, his entire body straining as he took her, as he sent her soaring higher. Her fangs descended when she saw his were down, a feral need rolling through her in response to the sight of them. She wanted to bite him. She groaned and threw her head back as he plunged into her, harder now, as if the sight of her fangs had excited him too, had pushed him over the edge. Callie tried to banish thoughts of biting him from her mind, but it was hard, the hunger constantly riding her as pleasure built inside her, as she reached for release.

She bounced on Rune's cock, focused on how good it felt inside her, how this wild moment with him was sating the urges that had come over her when she had seen him fighting, the need that had been steadily growing inside her from the moment she had met him.

Rune dropped one hand to her thigh, brushed his thumb over her soft folds and then her sensitive bead.

Callie cried out as pleasure detonated inside her, heat rolling through her on every powerful flex of her body around his cock. Her thighs quivered as she tried to keep riding him, as he continued thrusting into her and stroking her, quickly pushing her towards a second release.

It came upon her in a blinding flash as Rune roared and spilled inside her, his length kicking and throbbing, his hot seed pulsing into her. Her body greedily milked his, her breaths leaving her on stuttering sighs as she swayed with each one, as she clung to consciousness as a black tide rolled up on her.

Rune slumped beneath her.

Callie cracked her eyes open, caught a glimpse of his slack face before she sank against his chest, breathing hard as she listened to his heart thundering against her ear.

And there was her proof.

She stroked Rune's chest, waiting for him to come around, unsure what she was going to tell him when he woke. Gods, she hoped he knew less about wolf shifters than she thought so she could pass off his blacking out as something to do with exertion and the heat of the moment. She thought about what her mother had told her long ago, before she had died. So many wolves had tried to convince Callie that her mother had been lying, but now Callie knew she had been telling the truth.

Sex between two people who could share the most powerful of bonds could result in one or both of them passing out if the female was a wolf ripe for bearing a cub.

Callie pushed herself up and gazed down at Rune's face.

He was her fated one.

But would he want to be her mate?

CHAPTER 15

Birdsong filled the silence, heralding the arrival of evening as Rune and Callie followed a wide dirt track that wound through the woods, leading towards a sloping green meadow a few hundred feet away. Beside him, Callie fidgeted with the sleeve of her black hoodie, her amber gaze locked on it.

When he had come around in the glade to find Callie watching over him, she had done her damnedest to convince him he had blacked out from exertion. Rune wasn't buying it. It might have been decades since he'd had sex, but he had never been the sort to pass out, and something about the way Callie was acting around him now made him suspect she was lying to him.

Why?

He didn't like it when people lied to him, found he liked it even less when it was Callie spinning tales. The urge to press her to tell him the truth surged through him again but he denied it. The last time he had questioned her about what had happened, she had clammed up and then she had grown snappish when he had pushed her again.

Rune scanned the long sweeping stretch of greenery that ran from the mountain to his left to the taller bushes and trees that edged the river to his right, trying to focus on keeping an ear open and an eye out for potential danger. The last thing he needed was Carrigan sneaking up on him while he was distracted by what had happened.

Callie's pace picked up. He frowned at her and wanted to ask where she was going, but then he heard it too. He strode after her, towards the source of the sound of water. She disappeared around a bend, a steep wall of naked rock stealing her from view, and Rune growled as he hurried after her, the urge to keep her within his line of sight compelling him to run until he could see her again. He somehow managed to stop himself from sprinting after her like some panicked fool, kept tabs on her with his senses instead.

She had stopped a short distance around the corner.

Rune saw why when he rounded the rock that jutted out onto the track.

A stream tumbled down the mountain to his left, slicing through the dense bushes and babbling over the boulders that cut above the water in places. That water dropped a short distance up the incline, cascaded over bands of rock in a stunning waterfall that caught the evening light, causing a faint rainbow that hung in the still air. Rune tracked the falls to their starting point high up the mountain, where they dropped in a long stream down the sheer face of granite before hitting the gentle grassy slope that hugged the base of the cliff and running towards the greenery.

Callie sighed and looked around, a faraway look in her eyes. "Is there anywhere around here that isn't beautiful?"

Rune smiled at how in love with the area she sounded—about as in love with it as he was. "Want to rest here a while?"

She met that question with a vigorous nod and was quick to find a boulder to sit on, one that was on the opposite side of the track to the falls, close to where the stream ran across it to join the river behind her.

Rune parked himself on a rock opposite her, his back to the falls and his gaze on her. A feeling came over him again, a fierce, possessive hunger that he found difficult to deny, one that had only grown worse since they had made love.

Her gaze drifted to him, her dark eyebrows pinching and then relaxing as nerves shone in her eyes. He braced himself in response, aware she was going to ask him something and it was going to be something he didn't like. She always got nervous when she was afraid he might react badly to something.

"You have a lot of scars." She looked at the mountain and then back at him, but he could see she wanted to avert her gaze again.

Rune sighed. "You've seen maybe ten percent of them."

Thinking about the ones she hadn't seen had his mood darkening, had memories surfacing that he wanted to deny because he didn't want to ruin the calm that was growing between them.

For the first time in a long time, he felt comfortable around someone. The thought of wrecking it by revealing things that might create a divide between them or cause her to change her opinion of him was enough to have his temper flaring, even when being in a mood with her was the last thing he wanted.

Because it would only make it easier for him to screw everything up.

It would only make it more likely that she would start viewing him in a different light, one that wasn't so complimentary.

"You have that look in your eyes again," she whispered. "The same one you had when you saw Carrigan. Did he… Is he responsible for your scars?"

"Some of them," Rune grunted, and he wasn't talking just about his physical scars now. The biggest scar Carrigan had left on him had been emotional, and it was his worst one. "The rest of them came from the arena."

"Why do you hate Carrigan so much?" Callie lifted her left foot and pressed the sole of her boot to the rock, toyed with her laces as she looked at him.

Waiting.

He stared at her, his heart drumming faster, adrenaline swift to flood him as he considered doing something that would probably ruin what was happening between them.

But he needed her to know.

He needed everything out there, in the open, removing the weight of it from around his neck.

"Carrigan is a traitor. I'm pretty sure if everyone knew what he had done, that there wouldn't be a single wolf in this world who would do business with him. I'm pretty sure they'd kill him." Rune fixed his gaze beyond Callie, on the mountains that rose up on the other side of the valley, watching their white peaks changing colour as the sun began to set. "He was captured around thirty-five years ago, maybe a little more, but it was after the hunters brought Maverick to Vancouver."

"Maverick was made to fight in the cages too?"

Rune nodded. "He's a natural though. Unlike me, Maverick was born to fight. I've never seen anyone take to life in the arena like Maverick did."

"He didn't seem that—"

"What Maverick seems like and what he is are two very different things, Callie." He cut her off with a hard look, one that made her tense. Or maybe it was the harshness of his tone that had her shoulders going rigid beneath her black top.

He didn't mean to be brusque, but the thought of her making the same mistake many had before her flooded him with a need to fight and a need to protect her.

"Too many people in this world have thought Maverick harmless and they all paid the price. The turnover in the compound doubled the moment Maverick arrived. I love that bear, but he's dangerous and he's too easily seduced by the darker side of his personality." Rune rubbed the back of his neck, the skin where the hunters had marked him feeling hot beneath his fingertips as he thought about how life at the compound had changed with Maverick's arrival.

"That… Your ink. Does B stand for bear?" Callie glanced at him and then away, fidgeted with her bootlace again.

He huffed. "I was the eighty-second bear they caught. Maverick's number is in the two hundreds. Grace was 143-B."

"Grace?" Callie's eyes landed on him.

Rune averted his and stared at the mountain again, because while he might be a fighter, it turned out he lacked guts. He couldn't bring himself to look at Callie as he said this, didn't want to see the change that would take place in her eyes, some foolish part of him hoping that if he didn't look at her, that it wouldn't happen.

She wouldn't change her mind about him.

He wouldn't ruin things.

"Grace..." He sighed as he thought about her. "She was a Kermode bear. Petite. Pale hair and jade eyes. Too fragile for such a brutal place. I knew the moment I saw her that without help she wouldn't survive long. Whether it was in the arena or out in the communal areas of the compound, someone would have gotten too rough with her... so I stepped in."

Rune hardened his heart as images of Grace filled his mind, tried to let them bounce off him but each one was a spear in his heart, cutting him deeply.

"You protected her." Callie carefully said each of those words, drawing them out as her gaze drilled into his face. "You fell in love with her."

Rune closed his eyes.

Apparently, it was all the answer Callie needed.

"What happened to her?" she whispered, the softness of her voice offering him comfort and strength, even as it tore at his heart, ripping open the gashes that his memories of Grace had left in it.

"Carrigan happened." Rune flicked his eyes open and looked at Callie, needing her to see how badly he wanted Carrigan's head, how deeply he needed to avenge Grace and make the male pay for everything he had done—not only to him and Grace, but to everyone he had betrayed. He growled. "Carrigan learned quickly that if he sucked up to the hunters by feeding them information that they would take care of him. No fights he couldn't win. More freedom in the compound. Any female he wanted brought to him and served on a silver fucking platter."

"Grace," Callie breathed.

Rune snorted and then chuckled coldly. "Only Grace used everything I'd taught her to cut him up and came running to me and Maverick. I protected her and drove Carrigan away. She was distraught, but unharmed... but—"

He sucked down a deep breath, forcing it past his tight throat as memories of that night roared up on him, as they filled his mind and wrenched at his heart.

"But?" Callie prompted.

He exhaled hard.

Pushed the words out.

"Carrigan told the hunters about what he had seen. He wanted me to pay… maybe wanted Grace to pay too… for not wanting him. He told the hunters about us, that we'd been involved for a number of years, something which was strictly forbidden. No relationships. Flings and fucking were fine, but emotions softened us. Weakened us. Turned us into poor entertainment. The hunters wanted us sharp, hard and cold, like a blade." He scrubbed a hand over his face and pulled down another hard breath, his heart aching as he thought about what had happened. He couldn't bring himself to look at Callie, tipped his head forwards and closed his eyes, covering them with his hand. "The hunters… The hunters made me fight."

"Carrigan?"

He shook his head.

"There was a polar bear. Klaus. Huge bastard. Unbeaten. He had always wanted to fight me, but being two of the best fighters meant we were never matched together. The hunters wanted to keep their prized fighters alive. Klaus was given a shot at me, but on the proviso he didn't kill me." Rune rubbed at his eyes as they stung, swallowed hard and tried to clear the lump from his throat. "The hunters told me that if I won, Grace would be spared, and our relationship would be allowed to continue as long as it didn't interfere with my fights."

"And if you lost?"

Rune swallowed again.

Croaked.

"Grace would have to fight Klaus and I would be forced to watch."

"Gods, Rune," Callie murmured and he sensed her move, wanted to tell her to stay where she was but couldn't find his voice. She wrapped her arms around him, holding him to her, and he sank against her, his strength rushing from him as her scent and her warmth surrounded him and he realised that he hadn't ruined things between them.

His beautiful wolf still cared about him.

She stroked her hand over his close-cropped hair, the feel of it soothing him, stealing away his hurt.

Hurt that returned as she whispered, "What happened?"

He squeezed his eyes shut and let two words tumble from his lips.

"I lost."

He had been so confident going into the arena, too confident perhaps. Klaus had proven too strong for him even in his human form and no matter how desperately Rune had fought, the thought of Grace having to fight driving him to win, he hadn't been able to bring the polar bear down.

When the hunters had dragged him from the cage, he had been exhausted and in phenomenal pain.

But that pain had been nothing to the agony that had swallowed him when they had pushed Grace into the cage. Her terror had hit him hard, her pained and desperate cries as she had valiantly attempted to fight Klaus utterly destroying him.

By the time those cries had ceased, Rune had been a shell of a male. Empty. Numb. The next few weeks had been a blur of grief and rage, of polar moments of staring blankly into nothing and bloodying his hands in brutal fights. Maverick had tried to take care of him, and when that hadn't helped him, the grizzly had gone after Carrigan.

Only Carrigan had escaped, whisked away to another location by the hunters, placed beyond Rune's reach.

Until now.

Now, Rune would have the vengeance he needed.

He leaned back, breaking free of Callie's hold, and tilted his head up. She gazed down at him, her expression soft, her eyes revealing her thoughts to him—she thought he still had feelings for Grace. It was right there in that shimmer of hurt that wasn't pity for him.

He did, but not in the way he had.

Callie twisted away from him, her eyes on the sky.

An awkward edge to them.

Rune stood, dusted his backside down and stilled as he looked at her. "We should keep moving."

It wasn't what he had wanted to say. He had wanted to tell her that while he had loved Grace, he was no longer in love with her. Callie moved before he could find the courage to put those words out there, turned her back to him and crossed the stream that flowed over the track.

He heaved a sigh and followed her, some of the weight settling back on his shoulders as he tried to find a way to tell her and make her see she was wrong to think the things she was. That fight kept him silent as they walked, heading for a grassy stretch of land dotted with bushes. He had thought telling Callie about Grace would change her opinion of him, and maybe it had, but not in the way he had expected it. He had imagined she would look at him as if he was weak and unable to protect her, as if he wasn't worthy of her because he had already failed to protect another female under his care.

The edge to her eyes as she glanced over her shoulder at him, the flicker of hurt and confusion, and hopelessness, wasn't at all what he had expected. Mostly because it had confirmed she had feelings for him. She cared about him.

He cared about her too.

Callie stopped a few feet into the meadow and crouched. What was she doing? He closed the distance between them in a handful of strides and frowned down at her. She glanced up at him, the motion causing her to lean back slightly and reveal what she had been doing.

Picking flowers.

Small yellow blooms.

"Spring is definitely here then." Rune eased into a squat beside her and plucked one of the flowers from her hand. She stilled when he tucked it behind her right ear, hooking her black hair behind it, and looked at him, a confused crinkle to her brow. He smiled softly. "Glacier-lilies look good on you."

Smelled good too.

He liked to think his bear instincts didn't make him do crazy things like they did with Saint and the others, making them want to sleep through winter and such, but just the sight of the lily filled him with an urge to eat it.

He stood and held his hand out to Callie.

Froze when his senses detected movement.

Rune looked off to his right, deeper into the meadow, and narrowed his eyes on the grizzly that emerged from behind a bush to rake claws over a clump of the lilies, digging up their bulbs.

The brown bear lifted its head and sniffed the air, his lower lip hanging down, revealing his teeth.

Rune knew when it had caught his scent.

It groaned and swayed, and began walking towards them on stiff legs, every step overly pronounced. Posturing. The male was trying to threaten Rune, really wasn't happy to see him. He eyed it warily. It wasn't a bear he knew. It was a decent size for a young male, probably a few hundred pounds already, and was probably just caught up in the season, a slave to its instincts.

It saw Rune as a bear and wanted to brawl.

The grizzly jutted its head forwards and roared.

Rune moved in front of Callie and stood his ground as the animal kept advancing.

"Back off," he growled.

The bear did the opposite.

It charged him.

CHAPTER 16

Callie was still trying to process what Rune had told her about his life in Vancouver and about Grace, and how he had gently tucked a flower in her hair, was so caught up in her thoughts that the grizzly bear suddenly charging them startled her. The animal thundered towards her across the meadow, moving at speed, and she wasn't sure whether to stand her ground or attempt to move out of its path.

She had never been charged by a bear before.

Was she meant to remain still and look big, or run like hell?

Her gaze shifted to Rune, that question on the tip of her tongue.

He shocked her too by stripping off and shifting.

It wasn't seeing him naked that stunned her, or even the fact he had shifted to face off against an animal.

It was the fact he wasn't a grizzly bear.

Callie stared at Rune's rounded, furry backside, her eyes slowly widening as she tried to take in the fact he was a cinnamon black bear. His reddish-brown fur was lush and thick, covering his big body, and when he moved to stand side-on to the charging grizzly to reveal his size, she noticed his snout was tan, a slight contrast to the rich colour of his fur.

Rune roared when the grizzly didn't stop his charge and kicked off, thundering towards the bear. She flinched as they clashed, as both Rune and the bear rose up on their back legs and roared again as they struck each other with their large paws. The grizzly was far smaller than Rune, but that didn't stop it from trying to take him down. The bear attempted to bite him and Rune slapped it hard across the face, knocking it away. It landed on its side and was quick to get up again, to swipe and bat at Rune as he landed on all fours in front of it. Rune growled as he took a hit, the bear's claws catching his left front leg.

The one she and the wolf back at the ravine had both injured.

The roar he unleashed on the smaller bear echoed around the valley and the grizzly shrank back, took a hard blow from Rune's right paw again.

This time, the bear took the hint and turned tail, its furry backside jiggling with each stride it took. Rune chased it, smacked it on its bottom, and the bear loosed a mournful groan.

Callie shook her head as Rune finally gave up his chase, feeling bad for the grizzly and unimpressed with Rune. The bear had been leaving. It hadn't been necessary of Rune to chase it and humiliate it further by slapping it on its backside.

Rune stalked back to her and she frowned as she noticed he was limping slightly. She gathered his clothes and hurried to him, worry arrowing through her as she crossed the meadow to reach him.

She grimaced as she got close enough to see the blood causing glossy patches on the shorter reddish-brown fur that covered his left front leg, unsurprised that he had made his injury worse by running the bear off.

"Was that really necessary?" Callie dumped his clothes before him as he shifted back, the fur sweeping away to reveal pale golden skin as he rose onto his back legs.

Rune looked at his forearm and shrugged, stood there naked as the day he had been born. "The bear challenged me. What was I supposed to do?"

His pale blue eyes met hers, as serious as she had ever seen them, and she shook her head again.

"Oh, I don't know. Let him have his way? He was just a little bear." She picked up his jeans and tossed them at him, even when part of her was quite enjoying the view and didn't want him to steal it away from her. The sight of his incredible body was distracting her though, rousing that need that constantly simmered in her veins when she was around him.

He grunted and tugged his jeans on, a black look settling on his handsome face. "He charged you. I wasn't going to let him just charge you like that and not respond."

That was kind of sweet of him.

"I can handle myself." She ignored the voice that whispered she hadn't been handling anything. She had panicked and hadn't even known what to do when faced with a bear charging her. By the time she had figured it out, the bear would have been on top of her.

He frowned at her, his dark eyebrows knitting hard and narrowing his eyes as his lips turned downwards.

She stepped up to him, lifted her hand and gently brushed the pad of her thumb between his eyebrows, smoothing the deep furrow away. "But thank you for saving me."

His expression shifted, softening by degrees as he gazed down at her, right into her eyes. For a heartbeat, she thought he would kiss her, but then he stepped back and pulled his boots on, following it with his long-sleeved T-shirt. He picked up his fleece and clutched it in his right hand.

A hint of colour touched his cheeks as he glanced at her, his eyes quick to leap away from her again. He rubbed the nape of his neck and grunted something as he jerked his chin in the direction they had been going before the bear had decided to challenge him.

Awkward Rune was quite adorable.

She followed him as he started walking, her gaze drifting to him as he tugged the long sleeve of his T-shirt up his right arm and inspected the bite wounds on it. He huffed as he prodded one of the deeper welts, and then sighed and pulled his sleeve back down again to cover them. When they reached the other end of the meadow and entered another stretch of dense pine forest, she couldn't hold her tongue any longer.

"So… are we going to talk about the fact you're not a grizzly?"

Rune cast a glance at her. "I never said I was one."

"That's true, I suppose. I just thought… Since you called Maverick a grizzly… Are there any other black bears in your pride?" She was curious now, couldn't imagine Saint as a black bear, but thought perhaps Lowe and

Knox might be that breed. Although, while Lowe came off as laid back enough to be a black bear, Knox had the grizzly temperament.

"No. They're all grizzlies." Rune gestured with his right hand, pointing out a faint trail that led downwards in that direction, and she turned with him, following it.

The smell of water grew stronger and she could hear the river running. The fear that had disappeared when Rune had told her that Carrigan couldn't cross the river until he was close to the White Wolf pack returned, trickling through her veins as she realised they were almost at the point where they would finally be level with the river.

To take her mind off it, she said, "How did you come to be in a pride with grizzly bears?"

"I told you. Saint came to Vancouver around twenty years ago, together with some other bears and shifters, and they executed a raid on the compound where I was being held. Shut the place down pretty quickly." Rune pulled his fleece back on and she wanted to pick him up on the fact he hadn't told her that Saint had been the one to free him, but in the end she let it slide, because it was nice he was opening up to her, telling her more about himself. If she mentioned he hadn't told her these things, he would clam up again and probably lash out at her. "After we all escaped… well… Maverick talked to Saint and Saint offered us both a place in his pride."

"I thought…" She trailed off as she thought about the things he had told her and realised that again she had assumed something, because he had spoken of his family as being the bears at Black Ridge. But before that, he had told her that the White Wolf pack could be what Black Ridge was for him—a new family. She had thought he meant new for her.

He had meant new for him.

She studied his profile as they walked. "I thought you were all from the same pride."

The corner of his mouth twitched. "We are… now. The pride is around forty percent bears who were born into it and the rest are strays that Saint has picked up. Us strays… Maverick and me… Knox and Lowe… we stick around most of the year. The other seven bears tend to come and go. They have their own lives outside the pride and have homes elsewhere. It's rare for us to all be together at once at Black Ridge."

Callie ducked beneath a low branch of a young pine.

"Sounds like the White Wolf pack." She shrugged as his gaze landed on her, as she thought about that and about herself. "Guess I'm a stray too."

Rune looked as if he wanted to say something, but a noise coming from ahead of them had his pale blue eyes leaping towards it and narrowing. Callie cocked her head, listening hard to see if it would come again, because it had sounded a lot like a voice. Her heart drummed, blood rushing at the thought it might be Carrigan and his men.

Only the laughter that echoed quietly through the trees was feminine.

"Looks like we're here." Rune jerked his chin towards something as she glanced at him.

Callie looked there, peering past the trunks of the densely packed pines and spruces, trying to spot what he had. Dread pooled in her stomach, nerves replacing the fear in her veins as she caught a glimpse of a log cabin among the trees.

The White Wolf pack.

Rune must have sensed her nerves, because he gently laid a hand on her right shoulder and murmured, "They'll take you in, Callie. They'll give you the protection you need."

The thought they might reject her wasn't the reason she wanted to turn tail and run in the opposite direction. She shifted her gaze to Rune, stared into his eyes as a thousand things she needed to say to him leaped to the tip of her tongue, warring with each other to be said.

She was afraid he was going to leave and she would never see him again.

Crazy, she knew, but she feared it all the same. The fact she knew the way to Black Ridge wasn't a comfort to her either, had her imagining going there only to be openly rejected by him in front of all his pride.

"Rune—" she started.

"Who are you?" A young brunette female bounced into Rune's path, making him stop dead. Her bright green eyes assessed him as she sniffed. "You're not wolf."

Rune looked as if he might flash his fangs at her but then he grunted, "Came to see Rourke. Got a wolf in need of a home and protection."

Callie stepped forwards. "If you could just tell us where to find him."

The female shrugged and stepped back up onto the deck of the log cabin to Callie's left, and nudged the blue-jeans-clad thigh of a blond male. He snorted as he woke with a jolt and scowled at her, his folded arms falling away from his green checked shirt.

"Got a wolf here wanting to see Rourke, and a guy who looks like trouble." The female glared over her shoulder at Rune.

The male huffed and leaned to his left, peering past her. "That's a bear. Told you not to poke bears. You've got to put more effort in at school and learn to tell the difference between shifters, sis."

"Maybe if I didn't have to do all your chores on top of mine, I'd have time to study, lazy ass." She kicked him in the thigh again and then went inside the cabin.

He scowled at the door as it slammed and then sighed, gripped the arms of his wooden recliner and pushed onto his feet. "Come with me."

Callie stuck close to Rune as they trailed after the wolf, following a path marked by three-foot-high electric lamps that barely chased away the gloom. She looked up at the dense canopy above her, barely able to make out patches of the evening sky. The dirt path wound between closely-packed cabins and she peered down the paths that broke off from it, ones that led to even more cabins. There had to be thirty or forty of them beneath the trees. How big was this pack?

When the trail took them close to the river, she moved to that side and stared at the shallow rippling water and then at the other bank, where more cabins clustered together.

"You okay?" Rune grumbled.

Callie forced a nod, but she wasn't okay. She wasn't anywhere near it. Everywhere she looked, she saw more wolves, and it was setting her on edge. She hadn't managed to get a good look at a lot of the males who were accompanying Carrigan. Any number of them might be hiding in plain sight among the wolves milling around outside the small log cabins.

Rune closed ranks with her, his arm brushing hers, the scent of him filling her lungs to calm her together with the feel of him beside her. Nothing bad would happen to her. He would make sure of that. She knew it deep in her heart.

A clearing came into view ahead of them, the large firepit in the centre of it catching her eye. The flames flickered and leaped, sending sparks shooting into the air between the overhanging branches. She looked up as she reached the clearing and breathed deep as she gazed at the sky, soothed by the sight of it. Everything about this place felt claustrophobic, but this small spot was different. Wolves hung out in groups of two or three, talking as they went about their business, some of them coming and going from one of the larger cabins. The smell of food emanated from inside it.

Their escort quickened his pace and Callie tracked him with her gaze as he skirted around the fire to the other side. The largest of the cabins stood there, one that had to be twice the size of the others she had seen. The L-shaped affair had a wide deck that ran along the front and around the inside of the L, and beneath the overhanging roof of the porch of the façade, two large picture windows framed the open door.

The blond wolf took the two steps up onto the deck and poked his head into the building. He nodded and moved back and to one side.

A tall, handsome male with wild white hair and kind eyes stepped out onto the deck, rubbed his hands on a small cloth and strode down the steps. His dark jeans emphasised his long legs and a red-and-black plaid shirt hugged his chest, accentuating his athletic figure.

The white wolf himself.

She swallowed her nerves as he approached them, the firelight chasing over the sculpted planes of his face, bringing out the flecks of gold in his dark eyes.

"Was told you wanted to see me?" He tucked the cloth into his back pocket and looked from Rune to her.

Rune tensed and she swore she sensed anger in him, glanced at him and found him staring at Rourke with no trace of emotion in his ice-blue eyes.

He was angry though.

She could feel the barest undercurrent of it in him, knew him well enough to spot the subtlest of shifts in his mood now. He was angry with Rourke. Why? It dawned on her that it was because the male had looked at her.

"We have a tail," Rune said, his deep voice darker than she had ever heard it, even when he had been growling at her when they had first met. His features pinched, eyebrows knitting hard above his glacial eyes as he locked gazes with Rourke and stared him down. "Got an alpha after her and he has eight men with him. All looked like they can handle themselves."

He really didn't like Rourke. She thought about that and about what he had told her, and had the feeling it wasn't because he was surrounded by wolves and didn't like it. He just hated Rourke. He hadn't reacted badly to the young female or the male who had led them here. His mood had only taken a dark turn once he had seen Rourke.

Because Rourke was as handsome as Saint had said he was?

He might be good looking, but Rune was more handsome in her eyes.

"Sounds like trouble. We can handle it. Any information you can give me on the ones pursuing you might prove helpful though." Rourke's bass voice was smooth, even and calm, exactly how Saint had spoken with her. He was doing his best to defuse the situation and show Rune he wasn't the enemy, but Callie had the feeling it wouldn't work on her bear.

Her bear.

She looked at Rune, every fibre of her being screaming that he was her bear.

Her bear who grunted and spoke loudly enough that the entire world could hear him, intentionally raising his voice to ensure he was heard. "Alpha is a real asshole. Piece of shit who thinks he can do as he pleases with females just because he was born with a dick. Expects them to serve and please him. You know the sort."

Rourke's eyes darkened and his jaw flexed, but he proved just how diplomatic he was by not rising to the bait. "We get a lot of wolves coming here from such packs and all are welcome."

Rune didn't look happy and when he opened his mouth to launch another salvo at Rourke, she touched his arm, stealing his focus away from the wolf. He looked at her, the fire in his eyes fading as he gazed down into hers, as he lingered. She smiled softly, covering the hurt welling inside her as she looked into his eyes, as she thought about how little time she'd had with him and how she didn't want him to leave.

"What's your name?" Rourke said and she realised he was talking to her.

She glanced at him. "Callie."

Rourke nodded and signalled with his right hand, and a brunet male and a sandy-haired female came over to him.

"You must be tired, Callie. You look as if you've been through a lot, but you don't have to worry anymore. You'll be safe here. Let's get you settled and then we can talk more about your problem." Rourke looked at the two wolves. "Take her to lodge twenty-two. Make sure she has everything she needs."

She glanced at Rune, her brow furrowing as she found him staring at the fire, his head turned slightly away from her and his shoulders rigid. She touched his arm and willed him to look at her, but he kept his eyes on the flames. The air seemed to chill around her as she waited for him to acknowledge her, the cold sinking deep into her bones when she realised he wouldn't because he was building a wall between them again, bringing his barriers back up to shut her out.

"I'll just..." She wasn't sure what she wanted to say, couldn't find her voice as the hurt welling inside her grew more intense, stealing her breath and weighing her down.

The female wolf took hold of her arm and Callie stared back at Rune as she led her from the clearing.

Rourke shifted his dark gaze from her to Rune. "Come with me. I have a few questions I'd like to ask you about this alpha."

Rune nodded and followed him.

Didn't even glance at her.

Callie trudged along beside the female wolf, not really hearing her as she prattled on about life at the White Wolf pack and how much she was going to love it. The male trailed behind them, adding comments from time to time, and it was clear the two of them were an item. That only made her heart feel heavier.

"Here we are." The female opened the door of a small log cabin, one with an overhanging pitched roof and a small deck in front of the door and a single window.

It reminded Callie painfully of the one where Rune had held her the night they had met, deep in the woods on the mountain.

She tried to be polite as the female showed her around the cabin, excitedly pointing out the working bathroom facilities and the fact everyone had electricity here. It was nice.

But it didn't feel like home.

She looked over her shoulder at the door, an ache to see Rune forming in her breast as she reached out with her senses and couldn't pinpoint him with them.

Panic lanced her.

"I just—" She cut herself off, smiled and hurried from the cabin, running back towards the clearing as the ache to see Rune became an undeniable need, as fear whispered to her again.

Only this time, it didn't stop at telling her that he was going to leave and she would never see him again.

Her heart clenched as the reason for how distant he had been hit her like a lightning bolt, shaking her to her soul.

He was going to leave and go after Carrigan alone.

And he would get himself killed.

CHAPTER 17

"It isn't going to take Carrigan—" Rune cut himself off and pivoted to face the open door behind him as the scent of glacier-lilies hit him.

Callie came barrelling into the cabin, her eyes wild and a desperate look on her face, her fear hitting him hard.

Adrenaline shot through his veins and he was at her side in an instant, clutching her arms and searching her wide amber eyes.

"What's wrong? Is it Carrigan?" The thought that the male might have already reached the pack and found her shook him to his core, had his bear side restless and groaning, angry that he hadn't been there to protect her.

She breathed hard, shook her head, swallowed and looked as if she was struggling. Her hand came to rest against his chest, the soft warmth of her touch soothing him, and her too judging by how the crazed edge to her eyes faded and she began to relax.

"I just…" Her eyes darted between his, her hand trembling against his chest with the nerves he could feel in her. She flicked a glance at Rourke where he stood in the middle of the kitchen off to Rune's left and then her eyes locked with his again. Her nerves increased. "I… ah… I just thought I should be here too."

She was lying.

Rune could read in her eyes and in the way her fingers subtly moved against his chest, stroking him through his fleece, what she didn't want to say in front of Rourke.

She had been worried about him and had come running to him.

She had needed to see him.

He wasn't sure how to process that, or the way she made him feel, how tied in knots he was whenever he was around her, hoping for the first time in a long time for something.

Something he wasn't sure he deserved.

He was no gentle male. He was no Rourke, who had proven himself to be a decent kind of wolf in the short time they had been talking, discussing Callie and what her life here would be like, and the Carrigan problem.

Rune didn't know how to be like him, didn't know how to take care of a female. He barely knew how to take care of himself, and he even managed to screw that up sometimes.

He wasn't a good male, but the way Callie looked at him, her eyes soft with affection, with hope, with something a foolish part of him dared to believe might be the first seeds of love, made him want to be a better one. She made him want to put in the effort to learn, to adapt, and to overcome his past.

Because he was falling for her.

And he was falling hard and fast.

Every instinct he possessed roared at him that she was the one for him—the only one.

His true mate.

Her gaze darted downwards as he shifted his right hand to the curve of her waist, as he slipped his arm around her and turned so he was beside her and they were both facing Rourke. Her eyes leaped back up to meet his, the nerves in them fading, together with the fear that had laced her scent. Something akin to relief replaced them and the tension visibly drained from her.

"Make that coffee for three." Rune managed to smile at Rourke, making a valiant effort to be polite, something which was growing increasingly difficult again now that Callie was here.

The same primal instincts that told him Callie was something special to him, something once in a lifetime, also told him that Rourke and every unmated male in the vicinity were going to try to steal her from him.

Rourke proved how astute, and polite, he was by shrugging and keeping his eyes away from Callie as he went back to fixing them all coffee. Rune had the feeling he and Callie weren't the first fated but unmated couple to roll into his territory. Rourke handled it like a seasoned professional, didn't look at Callie once as he handed both her and Rune a mug of steaming coffee.

"You want milk?" Rourke set a small carton of it down on the counter near Callie. "Help yourself."

She smiled but Rourke didn't see it because he was already moving deeper into the cabin, towards an L-shaped couch that sat against the wall that divided the room into two down the middle, separating a small dining area from the living area. Rune waited while Callie made her coffee as pale as the milk she was pouring into it. He arched an eyebrow at her when she looked at him.

"What?" She scowled, but there was no malice behind it, only embarrassment she didn't need to feel.

"Just filing away that you *really* like milk in your coffee." He cracked a grin at her.

An alluring blush climbed her cheeks and she fidgeted with her mug, her eyes on the pale off-cream coffee. "I got really into lattes back at Revelstoke. There's a nice coffee shop there and I love to—Well, I guess… I loved to go there."

Her mood faltered, the light that had been filling her eyes winking out of existence.

Rune brushed his hand up and down her side, unsure what to say to comfort her and make her see that life here could be just as good as the one she had been torn away from, maybe even better. Probably because he didn't want her thinking about how great her life could be in this place. He didn't want her to stay here, so far away from him.

He wanted her as close to him as he could get her.

He felt Rourke's gaze on him, leashed the urge to growl at the male for making him feel rushed, and turned with Callie. "Let's get this talk over with. You look tired. Gods knows I've not let you get much sleep in the last twenty-four hours."

Rourke cocked a white eyebrow at that.

Rune glared at him, daring the male to even suggest he had been talking about keeping Callie up all night with sex. His mind took a wicked turn regardless, filled him with a hunger to do just that, to indulge her every whim, to pleasure her until he was the only male she would ever want and make her fall for him too.

Callie reached the couch before him and thankfully chose to sit at the end of it furthest from Rourke, allowing Rune to sit between them. He sank into the seat beside her and she angled her body towards him, tucking one leg up onto the couch as she nestled against his side. He looked at her as she told Rourke the same thing she had told him, adding a few more details that had him wanting to hunt down the alpha of her old pack and kill him too.

He must have looked ready to commit bloody murder when he looked at Rourke, because the white-haired wolf held his hands up.

"Not all alpha wolves are like that." Rourke's strange eyes—dark brown around the outside but green nearest his pupils—held a look that told Rune he didn't like how some alphas treated the females in their pack either. "Everyone is equal here, free to do whatever work pleases them, to train with the combat instructors and live the life they were born to. Hell, my second in command is female. You should probably meet her, Callie."

Rune barely bit back the growl that rumbled up his throat as the wolf leaned forwards to get a better look at her and dared to speak her name.

"Maybe in the morning." Rourke flicked him a look, one that said he had noticed how agitated he was. "It must have been a long journey for you both. I presume you're staying the night?"

Rune growled, "I'm staying until Carrigan is dealt with."

He wasn't sure what came after that.

Callie's gaze drilled into the side of his face and he looked at her, right into her eyes. That look was in them again—the one that made him want to stay.

The one that made him want a lot of things.

Like keeping her by his side, in his arms.

Like kissing her again.

"We should find you a place to bunk." Rourke sounded as if he wanted to get them out of his cabin before they started making out, was hurrying them along now, eager to get rid of them.

"He can stay with me." Those words leaving Callie's lips sent shock rolling through Rune.

Before he could convince himself she really had said them, she stood, stealing her delicious warmth from his side.

He glanced at Rourke. The male gave him a look, and Rune wasn't sure whether it was telling him to get going before she changed her mind or whether he didn't approve of the two of them sharing a cabin.

So he growled at him, baring his teeth for good measure.

Callie held her hand out to him and he took it, a jolt running up his arm as they made contact. When he stood, she didn't relinquish his hand. She kept hold of it as she led him outside. Rune shifted his hand in hers, interlinking their fingers, and marvelled at how soft her hand was against his and how she let him hold it like this.

He liked it.

He liked how comfortable he felt as they walked together, following the winding lamp-lit path through the woods, between small cabins that were dotted among the trees. All around him people talked in low voices and some laughed. The place had a nice vibe to it, one that felt far more social than Black Ridge, but that was understandable given how many people lived here, and how few people lived at his pride.

Black Ridge was quieter. Peaceful. But it had its rowdy times, more often recently since Saint had mated with the little cougar female, Holly. Now the barbecues had grown more frequent and the cougar pride came to them too. Every one of them felt like a gathering, a chance for people to talk about what they had been up to, discuss things about the valley they had noticed, or exchange news they had heard in town. It was beginning to feel more like this wolf pack did.

And Rune had found he liked it.

Being around other shifter breeds felt comfortable. It felt right. He knew why. The compound. He had always been around a mixture of shifter species there. Bears. Felines. Wolves. He had spent decades of his life in a strange sort of pride, and now his own pride was becoming like it. Black Ridge was no longer just bears. It was bears, cougars, and mortals.

Rune glanced at Callie.

He wanted to add a wolf to their ragtag pride.

In the distance, a loud cheer went up, and his senses locked onto that direction as he smelled humans. Rourke and his wolves had a thriving business here. Rune had noticed that a number of humans were moving around in an area downstream, one that looked as if it was beyond a tall wooden fence with a gate.

The White Wolf Lodge.

There were at least a dozen luxury cabins around three hundred feet away from the other side of that wall—a business run for unsuspecting humans who didn't know their hosts were wolf shifters.

Rourke had been right to build a high fence between the place where his wolves lived and his business, stopping the humans from realising what the staff who helped run the lodges were. Personally, Rune would have placed the lodges even further away from the fence than they already were. Hell, he wouldn't be risking everyone by running a business catering to humans in the first place.

Callie stepped up onto the deck of a small cabin and Rune stared at it, feeling uneasy. He didn't like that this was her home now. He didn't want her settling in here and thinking of this place as her new pack. He wanted to take her back to Black Ridge.

Needed to keep her close to him.

"What's on your mind?" Callie moved back to him when he didn't follow her up onto the deck and smoothed the pad of her thumb between his pinched eyebrows as she sighed. "You have that thinking look on your face again."

He muttered, "Do you like it here?"

She shrugged.

"It's too early to tell. I'm not sure though." She tilted her head back, her voice softening and growing distant as she stared at the trees that sheltered the cabins. "It seems so dark and closed in, and I can't see the mountains."

She dropped her head and smiled at him, hitting him hard in the chest with it.

"I think your valley is more beautiful."

He thought she was beautiful.

An urge to tell her that she didn't have to live here swept through him, the strength of it stunning him.

Did he really want her to live with him?

Rune stared at her and it hit him that he did. He needed this female far more than he had suspected, didn't want to be apart from her for even a second. For the first time in a long time, he felt as if he was mending, as if his future was brighter than his past, and he knew it was because of her.

"Rune?" she whispered, a little frown creasing her brow. "What's—"

He grabbed her and tugged her to him, cutting her off with a kiss. She instantly melted into him, wrapped her arms around his neck and held him to her, and gods he liked how she did that. He loved how fierce and demanding she was, and how she didn't shy away from his kiss. She tried to dominate him instead, rousing his passion and a need to battle her for control.

Rune seized hold of her waist, stepped up onto the deck and walked her backwards as he kissed her harder, as need rolled through him, cranking him tight inside with every step closer they came to the door of her cabin.

A wolf howled.

He tensed.

Callie broke away from him, her eyes wide, her fear drumming in his veins too.

Rune growled.

"Carrigan."

CHAPTER 18

Callie resisted when Rune tried to push her into the cabin. He shot her a glare, but she stood her ground, tensed every muscle in her body as she gripped the doorframe, refusing to let him lock her away. She wasn't a weak female. She was a fighter.

The hard edge to his eyes softened towards fear.

Fear she could feel in him as he stared at her.

Fear she knew the source of and wanted to tell him that everything would be fine.

He wouldn't hurt her by accident while lost to the side of him that had been born during his brutal captivity.

The part of her that didn't want to hurt him, that hated seeing that fear in his eyes, wanted to do as he desired and lock herself in the cabin, but she couldn't. She couldn't hide from Carrigan. This was her fight too and she needed to be in the thick of it, shaping her future with her own hands, winning her freedom.

And she needed to keep an eye on Rune too.

The thought of him fighting twisted her stomach in knots, and the fear it caused in her would only drive her mad if she let him have his way and she couldn't see that he was all right. Thoughts of him being injured—or worse—would torment her the entire time she was hiding.

Not only that, but she would be constantly expecting Carrigan to burst into the cabin and capture her.

Callie clung to that as an idea struck her—a way of making Rune relent and accept her presence in this fight.

"Carrigan knows my scent. What if he finds me holed up in this cabin during the fight? Or his men find me? I'll have no way of escaping them. Surely it's better to keep me close to you where you know I'm safe?" She pressed her hands to his chest and felt his heart thundering against her palms as his handsome face darkened once more. He didn't like that she was manipulating him like this, convincing him to do the opposite of what he really wanted, but she wasn't about to apologise for it. She wanted to be out there, keeping an eye on him, fighting her own battle. "We can protect each other if we're together, Rune."

He heaved a sigh, a look crossing his features that was hard to make out, and part of her expected him to lay down the law as he had before when they had talked about her fighting.

Only he didn't.

He grabbed her hand and tugged her with him, running back in the direction they had come, towards the clearing and Rourke's cabin.

Her heart raced, blood rushing as she caught Carrigan's scent in the night breeze and heard a commotion ahead of them. Raised voices echoed around the woods, drawing wolves from their cabins, most of them male. A few of them joined her and Rune, running for the clearing.

Rune kept her pinned to his side when they reached it, his grip on her hand tightening as they pushed through the wolves who had gathered there and were blocking their path.

"She belongs with my pack," Carrigan growled and her heart jacked up into her throat, lodging and trembling there as she waited to hear Rourke's response.

It was Rune who snarled, "Go to Hell, Carrigan. Callie isn't going anywhere with you."

Her gaze leaped to him, her heart warming as he glanced at her, a wealth of affection and fear in his eyes as they pushed through the last of the people who formed a semicircle around their alpha's cabin, hemming in Carrigan and his men. She shifted closer to Rune, feeling his strength flowing into her as her nerves rose to swamp her, as fear attempted to rattle her and make her want to turn tail and start running.

No.

She wouldn't.

This thing with Carrigan ended here.

She was done running.

Rourke folded his arms across his chest and his red-and-black plaid shirt stretched tight over his muscles as he stared down at Carrigan. The male stood with his eight men at his back, forming a wall between their alpha and the wolves of Rourke's pack.

Carrigan flashed fangs as he spoke. "You know you can't keep her. She doesn't belong to you."

Rourke's right eyebrow arched at that.

Fire surged through Callie and she had taken a hard step forwards before she had even noticed what she was doing.

"I don't belong to anyone!" she barked. "I'm not your property, Carrigan. I'm a person. I'm free to make my own choices."

Carrigan turned dark eyes on her, ones that shone amber in their depths. "Your alpha gave you to me. That makes you my property, *bitch*."

"Call her that again and see how fast I put you in the ground, asshole," Rune snarled and stepped up beside her, surprising her by not stepping in front of her to shield her.

Warming her.

He was right about bears. They did things differently. Now that he had accepted that she wanted to fight, he was going to stand by her side. He wasn't going to treat her as if she was weak, shielding her with his body to protect her from physical harm or to keep her gentle sensibilities from being hurt by witnessing a conflict. A wolf male would have done those things, holding her back, but not Rune.

Rune trusted she could fight her own battles, was going to provide backup for her and maybe a little muscle and fighting skill she was badly going to need. He might think she was a strong, capable female, and she was, but she also wasn't stupid. Rune was a bear, a powerful warrior, and she wasn't going to start burning her bra and turning down his help, thinking she could handle this alone. She needed him in this fight. She would be relying on his strength and prowess from the start.

She was going to be the backup.

Carrigan's gaze drilled into her, darkening by degrees, and his men grew restless as they began to eye the wolves who surrounded them. The blond male removed his green jacket and shoved it at one of his men, who fumbled with it as Carrigan released it and turned back on Rourke.

"Last chance, White Wolf," Carrigan growled, the amber in his eyes brightening as he narrowed them on Rourke.

"She's not mine to hand over…" Rourke shrugged "and she's not yours either."

The look that had been emerging on Carrigan's face, a sly smile that had revealed he thought he had won and Rourke wouldn't stop him from taking her back, disappeared into a scowl.

Rune flexed his fingers against the back of her hand and she could sense the tension in him increasing. Hell, the tension in every male present jacked up, and she drew down a breath, knowing this was it.

It was about to come down to a fight.

"Callie is right. She's her own person. She's not property. She's free to choose where she wants to be and who she wants to be with." Rourke tipped his chin up, coolly holding Carrigan's gaze.

"Your mistake." Carrigan sneered at him.

Callie wasn't prepared for how everything suddenly sprang into motion, was knocked backwards as a big blond male launched at Carrigan and both of them smashed into Rune. Rune growled and released her, grabbed Carrigan and landed a fierce blow on his jaw. Callie locked gazes with Carrigan, her eyes widening as his narrowed on her, the hunger in them turning her stomach.

For a heartbeat, everything went still, and then she was shoved further from Rune as a brawl broke out, pushed ever outwards towards the edge of the group as every male in the vicinity tried to get in on the action.

Including Rourke.

The white-haired male leaped into the fray, his lips peeling back off his fangs as he snarled and hurled himself off the raised deck of his cabin, landing on the back of one of Carrigan's men.

Someone grabbed Callie and she growled and went to slam an elbow into their face, stopped at the last second as she met the wide brown-to-green eyes of a pretty white-haired female who looked close to Callie's age.

"Rourke told me that if shit went down, I had to get you out of here." The female tugged her backwards, away from the fight. "Not because he's all about squashing your lady liberties like, my brother isn't like that, but because he figured a brawl between a bear and a bunch of wolves might get nasty, and… I think there was something about him not wanting said bear biting his head off if you got hurt."

Callie hated the distance that yawned between her and Rune. It ate at her soul, had fear drumming in her veins to steal her strength and fill her head with doubts that she would ever see her bear again. A war erupted inside her, tearing her between going with the female as Rourke had ordered and immediately disobeying her new alpha.

"I'm Jessie by the way."

Callie didn't care who she was. Resolve flowed through her, quick to defeat the side of her that wanted to be a meek little wolf, a good wolf, and obey her new leader so she didn't end up kicked out of the White Wolf pack. She knew Rourke meant well, as his sister had said, and that he was only trying to protect her, and himself, but she needed to fight.

It was hard to shake off over a century of following the rules, of obeying orders she didn't agree with, but the thought of Rune out there fighting Carrigan gave her the strength she needed.

She wasn't going to leave Rune to fight Carrigan alone. This was her fight too. She silently apologised to the female and then went through with her original plan, slamming her elbow into Jessie's face and catching her off guard. Jessie grunted and lost her grip on Callie, and Callie kicked off, racing back towards the clearing.

With Jessie hot on her heels.

Callie put in a burst of speed and banked left when she found the route blocked by agitated wolves all trying to see what was happening. She would have to go around and find another route into the clearing. Hell, she would go over the damned cabins if she had to, or through one at least. There had been a door at the back of Rourke's cabin as well as the front. She could use that to reach Rune.

She took a right, heading for it.

Her gaze snagged on a tall black-haired male who leaned against a thick post on the deck of a cabin to her right, a disinterested look in his golden eyes as he watched her approaching.

"Stop her," Jessie hollered.

Callie's heart shot into her throat as she realised the female was talking to him and fear that he might do as Jessie had asked rushed through her. She couldn't let him stop her from reaching Rune, and if he got his hands on her it would be game over. She was strong enough to fend off a female, but this male looked to be a different matter entirely. There was a darkness about him, an aura that had her instincts labelling him as dangerous, despite his slender build.

She needn't have worried though, because he merely watched her run right past him, not moving a muscle.

"Osiris!" Jessie snapped and Callie sensed her slowing as the male answered.

"You really want me to fight? You know what happens when I fight."

Ominous words if ever Callie had heard them.

She glanced back to find Jessie had stopped before Osiris and was looking up at him, her expression torn. Something was off about the black-haired wolf, seriously off. He smelled wrong. Like wolf, but with an undernote of something else. Something that had her hackles rising and an urge to get far away from him coursing through her. She left him to Jessie, hoping Osiris would prove a big enough distraction for the female that she could lose her.

Callie faced forwards again, sprinting harder, her senses locked on the battle to her right, beyond the cabins. She glanced down every path between them, cursing when she found all of them blocked either by spectators or people involved in the fight.

Ahead of her, Rourke's cabin came into view.

She ran for it, her eyes on the back porch.

Grunted as someone barrelled into her, knocking her down. Panic lanced her, adrenaline shooting into her veins as she recognised their scent from the pass. It was one of Carrigan's men.

He grabbed her by her hair, fisting it hard, and dragged her onto her feet. Callie willed the shift, aware she was going to need to be in her wolf form to take him down. He clucked his tongue and seized her right arm, twisted it hard enough behind her back that she cried out and fire blazed through her, the pain halting her shift before it had even begun.

Damn him.

She threw a wild look around her, trying to figure out how to escape him.

A shiver bolted down her spine, freezing her solid as she caught another scent.

"Good work," Carrigan drawled and movement off to her right drew her gaze there. He smiled coldly as he moved into view, wiping the knuckles of his left hand across his split lip to clear the blood away. His amber eyes were bright, flooded with hunger as he stared at her. "The others are keeping the dogs busy. Hand her to me. I will take her from here."

Callie looked from him to a third male who joined them.

She might have stood a chance if it had only been Carrigan, but she couldn't take on three males alone.

She was going to need help.

Callie screamed.

"Rune!"

Carrigan growled and struck her hard.

The world went black.

CHAPTER 19

"Rune!"

A chill shot down Rune's spine as he heard Callie scream his name and he grunted as the male he had been fighting slammed a hard right hook into his jaw, knocking him off-balance. His heart lurched into his throat, painfully beating there as he dodged the dark-haired wolf's next punch and smashed his fist into the male's stomach. The wolf doubled over and Rune shoved him away, into a group of Rourke's men.

Rune scoured the clearing for Callie, his senses stretching far around him as a desperate need to feel her, to find her, blazed through him.

Only he couldn't sense her anywhere.

There were too many people around him, all of them muddying his senses enough that he couldn't pick her out—if she was even near him. The dreadful weight that settled in his chest said that she wasn't, said he knew the reason she had called out to him, and he got all the proof he needed when he scoured the battle and realised he couldn't sense Carrigan either.

The bastard had slipped away and got his hands on her.

Gods, it was all his fault, he should have kept hold of the slippery bastard and killed him when he'd had the chance, but the male was wily, had used his men to overpower Rune.

Giving himself a chance to escape and reach Callie.

"Rourke!" Rune barked, placing half the blame on the white-haired male.

When Rune had realised he had lost sight of Callie, had grown frantic to find her, the wolf alpha had noticed and confessed he had ordered his sister to steal Callie away from the battle. If she had stayed at his side as he had intended, he could have kept an eye on her. He could have protected her. Rourke had meant well, but by trying to protect Callie, he had placed her in grave danger.

Rourke grabbed a brunet male by his hair and shoved his head down as he brought his knee up, smashed it into his face and knocked him out. His amber-lit gaze sought Rune as he shoved the unconscious male away from him, a flicker of worry in it.

Another male barrelled into Rune's back and Rune growled as he elbowed him in the face, pummelling him with it until blood burst from the male's nose and he released him, staggering backwards and howling in agony.

One of Rourke's men was quick to leap on him, taking over as Rune pushed and shoved his way towards Rourke.

"Carrigan has Callie," Rune snarled as he reached the white-haired male.

His eyes widened and he breathed, "Jessie."

"Might have her too. I'm about to find out. Going to track that bastard down and put him in the ground once and for all." Rage simmered in Rune's blood, had the instincts he had honed in the cage veiling his vision in red, clouding his mind with a hunger to fight and to kill. He fought to hold it together, fearing that if he let the battle hunger take him that he would end up hurting Callie too. He would never be able to live with himself if he did.

Rourke wildly scanned the fray, looking for something. Or maybe someone. His gaze stopped on a towering male with short blond hair and bright blue eyes.

"Anders!" Rourke signalled to him and the male looked at him, still gripping the throat of one of Carrigan's men. "You and Griffin handle this."

Anders nodded, a grim look settling on his sculpted features as he shifted his gaze back to the male he held in a death grip.

Rune shoved through the crowd, pushing for freedom, his heart drumming faster as the feeling that every second counted rose inside him. He didn't know where Carrigan's pack was located, might never find Callie if the bastard was able to escape. At the very least, he would be forced to waste time by going to her pack and beating the shit out of her old alpha until he told Rune the location of Carrigan's pack.

The gods only knew what Carrigan might have done to Callie by then.

Fear pounded inside him, a driving force that had him sprinting the moment he was clear of the fight, his senses scanning the route ahead of him as he inhaled deeply, trying to catch her scent. The strong odour of spilled blood overpowered everything and despair mounted inside him, the fear that he might be too late to save Callie rising to tear down all hope.

And then he smelled it.

Glacier-lilies.

Rune tracked the scent past several cabins, Rourke hot on his heels. He could sense the male's worry as it mingled with his own and was thankful that Rourke kept quiet, not distracting him from tracking the faint scent he hoped would lead him to Callie.

Prayed would lead him to her.

As they reached the edge of the cabins, he realised they were heading back towards Black Ridge.

And he caught the scent of Carrigan's blood.

Rune growled and broke into a sprint, switching to using his senses now he was free of the cabins, and Rourke kept pace with him.

"Ahead. I feel something." Rourke glanced at him.

Rune nodded. "I feel it too."

It was Callie and Carrigan and they weren't alone. He could sense two other males with them, bringing up the rear. Carrigan meant to use them to cover his escape, a distraction for him and Rourke that would slow them down. He looked at Rourke.

"Go," Rourke said. "I'll handle them."

Rune wanted to thank him, swore he would later once Callie was safely back in his arms. He focused ahead of him, beyond the two males as he and Rourke caught up with them, his senses locked on Carrigan as he ran with Callie held over his shoulder. The way her head lolled and bounced with each step and the fact she wasn't fighting Carrigan told Rune everything he needed to know.

The son of a bitch had knocked her out.

Rage poured through him, had reddish-brown fur sweeping over his skin as he sprinted harder.

"Carrigan!" Rune yelled, charging him.

Carrigan looked over his shoulder and ran faster for a few strides before he changed tack and stopped, turned to face him and tossed Callie aside as if she was trash.

Rune stared him down, refusing to slow as his instincts got the better of him. The look in Carrigan's eyes said the male knew how this was going to go down. They might not have a cage around them, but this was a fight to the death and it was going to be done in their human forms, just as it would have been in the arena.

Carrigan was ready for him when Rune barrelled into him, caught him and grappled with him, reared his head forwards and struck hard, cracking his forehead off Rune's. Pain blazed across the front of his skull, dampening his senses, but Rune weathered it, growled and grabbed him by his throat, squeezing hard as he drew his other fist back.

The wolf swept his arm up, knocking Rune's aside, throwing his blow off course, and then seized Rune's wrist and twisted hard. The bone in his arm burned, the pain blinding as the wolf tried to break it, and Rune snarled as he brought his knee up and slammed it into Carrigan's balls.

Grinned as the male grunted and staggered backwards, breaking away from him.

"You never did have any honour," Carrigan growled.

Rune scoffed. "Honour? You're going to lecture me about honour? You sold your own kind out. You killed Grace."

"You killed Grace," Carrigan countered and Rune bared fangs at him. "You killed her. You weren't strong enough to protect her, and now you won't be strong enough to protect this bitch either… and when you're dead and she's mine—"

Rune launched at him on a deafening roar, the thought of Carrigan touching Callie like that, of her being at his mercy sending an inferno blazing through his blood that blinded him, stole control and had him unaware of what he was doing. He was a slave to the violence that seethed inside him, knew only the taste of blood and the scent of it, only the burn of bones bruising beneath hard blows and the satisfying crack of his fists breaking them in return.

His own grunts filled his ears as the red haze descended, as he surrendered to the darker side of him, giving himself over to it, revelling in the pained cries that echoed in his ears.

Awareness came and went, rolling like high waves, revealing snippets of his actions on each great fall before he was swept up again. He growled as he gripped Carrigan's throat. Snarled as claws raked over his chest. Grinned as blood burst from a wound, spraying him. Primal instinct roared at him to keep going, pushed him through the burn of pain and exhaustion as he clashed hard with his enemy.

He twisted and slammed the male into the grass, struck him again and again, lost in the hunger for more, fighting to claw himself back from the darkness that writhed in his mind, goading him into keeping going.

The scent of lilies reached him above the foul, tinny odour of blood and he stilled, blinked as sweat stung his eyes, dripped from his chin and drenched his back.

Or maybe that was blood.

Rune stared down at what he had done, looked away as he saw the state of Carrigan, bile rising up his throat. Fear gripped him, had him wildly looking for the source of that light intoxicating fragrance that had brought him back, shattering the hold the darkness had on him.

Callie.

Sickness swept through him as he scanned the gloomy night, the thought he might have hurt her while lost to the darkness, that he might have killed her too, seizing his heart in an iron grip that made it feel as if it might burst and squeezing the air from his lungs.

She wasn't where Carrigan had thrown her.

That whole area was drenched in blood; the grass churned from the battle that had taken place.

Gods no.

He looked over his right shoulder as something moved behind him, every muscle in his body tightening in preparation as he tried to harden his aching heart, afraid of seeing what he had done.

Rourke kneeled on the grass a short distance away, hovering over Callie.

An unharmed Callie.

Rune sagged forwards, all his strength leaving him as relief poured through him. He tried to stand but his knees gave out.

Rourke looked as relieved as Rune felt as he glanced at Rune and then dropped his gaze back to Callie and said something to her.

Rune pushed to his feet, managing it this time, denying his trembling muscles and the pain that tore through him with each step. He needed to see Callie. That need gave him the strength to keep moving, had him edging ever closer to his beautiful wolf.

"You good?" Rourke looked him over and then dropped his amber-lit gaze back to Callie. "I thought it best to move her."

Rune fell to his knees beside her. "Thank you."

Rourke shrugged it off. "Thank you… for removing the threat to her."

Rune wanted to tell him that he hadn't killed Carrigan for her sake, but it hit him that he had. He had thought he wanted closure, had wanted to avenge Grace, but in the end, keeping Callie safe and stopping Carrigan from ever getting his hands on her again was what had driven him to kill the male.

Callie moved, her nose wrinkling, and her eyes fluttered open.

He had done it because he was in love with her.

Her amber eyes met his and then drifted to Rourke as the white-haired wolf helped her onto her feet.

"Let's get you back to your cabin." Rourke began walking with her and Rune realised they weren't alone now.

A black-haired male and a female with white hair stood just beyond Rourke.

"Jessie." Rourke handed Callie over to her. "Make sure she has everything she needs."

Jessie nodded and helped Callie back towards the cabins. Rourke lingered, his eyes on the male now, tension building in the air as something passed silently between them, and then followed her. The black-haired male watched them go and then sighed and headed down the sloping meadow, towards the river to Rune's right.

Rune stared after Callie, unsure what to do.

The threat to her was over and he had closed the door on his past. Some part of him said he should return to Black Ridge now, but he couldn't.

Not without Callie.

His fight wasn't over yet.

He was about to face his toughest one yet.

CHAPTER 20

Callie turned away from the door as Jessie exited through it, exhaled and let the tension flow from her tired muscles. It was over. Carrigan was dead according to the petite wolf who had been quick to paint a savage and brutal picture of Rune and the battle that had taken place.

Rune.

The weight she had been trying to shift from the moment she had heard Carrigan was dead and the threat to her was gone returned, pressed heavily upon her heart and had her pacing away from the door, unsure what to do.

Were things between her and Rune over now?

Carrigan was gone, Rune had avenged Grace and himself, and he had the closure he had wanted. Some wretched part of her kept whispering that he would leave now, would be on his way and she would never see him again. She tried not to listen to it, clung to the voice inside her that said Rune wanted her, that he had done this for her too, and that what she felt beat inside his heart too.

She refused to believe anything else.

Rune might have barriers around his heart that were layers upon layers of ice and razor-wire, designed to keep everyone out and protect himself, but he had let her see through that cold façade, had shown her the warm heart that he was shielding, and she believed it was because he felt the same way about her as she felt about him.

He was falling for her too.

Callie sighed, walked into the small kitchen area and washed her face and hands, the cool water soothing against her overheating skin. She idly went through the cupboards although she wasn't sure what she was looking for. She ended up taking out a mug and finding a packet of herbal tea that was still in date, and filled the kettle.

Stared at it as it boiled.

The door of the cabin opened and she assumed it was Jessie come to bring her the fresh linen and other things she had promised, only it wasn't a feminine voice that echoed Callie's thoughts as she stared at the mug and the kettle.

"What are you doing?" Rune's deep voice rolled over her, snapping her out of her reverie and startling her a little.

Her head whipped towards him and she blinked. "Settling in."

She guessed.

She wasn't really sure what she was doing. She had been moving on autopilot, lost in her thoughts, and had somehow ended up standing in the kitchen making tea.

His handsome features darkened, his eyebrows knitting hard above icy eyes as he looked at her, as he rubbed the back of his neck and averted his gaze, dropping it to the kettle. She noticed he had washed up, that the blood that had covered him was gone now, leaving only cuts and bruises behind, and he had swapped his fleece for a clean black T-shirt.

He glanced from the kettle to her and back again as he scratched his nape. "Guess this is it then?"

She swallowed her aching heart, lost her grip on her resolve as the voice she didn't want to listen to howled so loud that it drowned out the other one.

Callie shrugged.

Hated that he was going to leave.

He frowned at her, something crossing his eyes, and then he turned and walked out of the door.

Damn him.

She hurried after him, her heart in her throat now, the instinct to stop him and demand that he stay with her driving her, overpowering the voice of fear as it howled at her to force him into submission. He was her fated one and she was damned if he was just going to walk out of that door and out of her life.

Rune stopped in the middle of the path in front of the steps to her deck and pivoted to face her. "I have just one thing I need to say before I go."

Callie stilled and stared at him, pulse drumming faster, fear and hope colliding inside her as his face set in grim lines and he stomped back to her.

He stopped on the step below her, captured her cheeks in his palms and kissed her.

The softest, tenderest kiss she had ever experienced.

Warmth stirred in response to it, a lightness filling her that chased away her fear, that strengthened her hope as it silenced that wretched voice, and she sank into the kiss a little, wanting to believe he was trying to tell her what she really needed to hear, but was like her.

Afraid to do it.

Afraid to be the one to take the first step and confess he felt something for her.

Afraid that those feelings would go unrequited.

Rune dropped his hands to her hips, and for a moment she thought he would gather her to him, but then he hesitated and drew back.

Stared deep into her eyes.

Callie looked him over, the cuts on his face and his arms tearing at her, making her want to guide him indoors to take care of him. She feathered her fingers over his shoulder, ghosted them over a particularly nasty gash on his deltoid that had bled through his T-shirt, her brow furrowing as she thought about what Jessie had said to her.

As she thought about how hard Rune had fought.

For her.

She could see it in his eyes. They weren't cold. The look in them seared her, set her aflame, revealing how much he wanted her and how afraid he had been.

"You said a lot." Her voice trembled and she cleared her throat, even though she knew it was too late and he had already sensed the nerves in her. "I'm afraid I didn't really understand any of it though."

He scratched his nape again, cast his gaze away from her and then sighed and locked eyes with her again. "I'm not good at this."

Callie cursed herself, feeling bad and wanting to take back what she had said because she knew how difficult this kind of thing was for him, how hard it was for him to be like others. Like her. Although, she wasn't great at talking either. Rather than talking to him about her feelings, taking the leap and risking the fall, she had almost let him walk out of her life.

Rune swallowed hard and brushed his thumb against her waist as his eyes searched hers. "Do you think you'll be happy here?"

She stroked his shoulder, battling the urge to demand he let her tend to his wounds, aware that now wasn't the time to lay down the law with him like that. Now was the time to lay down the law about him leaving. He had fought for her, and now it was time she fought for him.

"Maybe." She gave a little shrug. "I won't know until I try it."

She didn't want to try it. She cursed herself again. Why couldn't she just tell him that she was crazy about him? That she was falling for him and it wasn't just because he was her fated one?

He cleared his throat. Awkwardly.

"Maybe… you'd be happy… with a different pride?"

Callie mock-frowned. "A different *pride?*"

She knew he was awkwardly asking her to come back with him to Black Ridge, but she wanted to hear him say it. She needed to hear him say it.

"I was thinking… maybe… my cabin is big enough for two." He placed his other hand against her waist again and she felt terrible when she noticed they were both trembling.

Callie eased closer to him, wanting to reassure him that he didn't need to be afraid, and tried to resist teasing him, but her mouth had its own ideas.

She smiled softly. "You only think your cabin is big enough for two?"

"No. I mean, my cabin is big enough for two and I know it's not fancy like this place, and it needs some work, and we don't have any wolves, but if you'd like to… I'd like you to…" He grunted and huffed. "I'm no good at this."

When he released her and turned away, scrubbing the back of his close-cropped hair, she didn't just feel bad. She felt terrible.

Callie caught his arm, stopping him. "I'm sorry. I just… I'm nervous. A little afraid. Humour in the face of fear and all that."

He glanced over his shoulder at her. His look softened and he turned back to her, lifted his right hand and brushed his palm across her cheek as his gaze seared her, warming again. Because she had admitted that she sucked in her own special way? Or because she had admitted that she was scared too?

He wasn't alone.

She wanted to be with him so much, but she was so afraid it wouldn't happen that she was in danger of ruining it, of actually stopping it from happening by doing everything wrong.

"I like the look of Black Ridge. I like you… It's just…" She sighed and placed her hand against his chest, over his heart, and stared there. "This thing with Grace."

Rune pressed a finger to her lips. "I loved Grace, but that was a long time ago, Callie… and what I felt for her… it doesn't even come close to what I feel for you. I'm far from perfect… I don't deserve someone like you… but I want you to live with me."

"Is that all you want?" She searched his eyes again, holding back her smile when his eyebrows pinched, a crease forming between them. "There's nothing else you want to ask me?"

She leaned towards him and gently stroked her fingers down his nape, relished the way he shuddered and his eyes widened even as they darkened, his pupils dilating to devour the ice-blue of his irises.

"You know?" he husked.

"I know." She stroked his nape again, holding his gaze. "I figured it out a while back… Confirmed it after the bridge incident."

His lips parted, the shock that rolled across his handsome face in danger of bringing her smile out. A frown was swift to follow it.

"I knew it wasn't exertion. I knew I hadn't passed out because I hadn't had the strength to keep going," he growled, and she knew it was all for show.

He wasn't angry with her for keeping it from him. She couldn't feel even the barest trace of that emotion in him. In fact, he felt calm. Happy? Glad that she knew they were fated and he didn't have to broach the subject?

Callie sidled a little closer, draping her arms around his neck as she canted her head to her right and smiled coyly at him. "If you wanted to maybe test that theory that you could keep going, you're welcome to come inside. My money is on you passing out again… Want to take that bet and prove me wrong?"

He growled again, flashing fangs as heat blazed in his eyes.

They dropped to her lips.

"Am I going to pass out every time?" He looked wary, his words carefully weighed as he gazed at her mouth, and she could feel how badly he wanted to kiss her.

Or maybe she just really wanted to kiss him.

"Not necessarily." She lured him a little closer, careful to avoid brushing his injuries, some part of her aware now really wasn't the time to be contemplating being intimate with him while the rest of her howled to take her mate, her male, and make him hers.

"A wolf mate thing?" he husked, his gaze growing hooded, still locked on her lips.

"Uh-huh," she mumbled, beginning to feel a little lost as she ached with anticipation, her mind filling with fantasies of him kissing her, of him bending her to his will this time. She shivered in response to them, her blood heating, body craving his touch.

"So we mate and no more blacking out?"

Gods, that question made her want to growl, made her want to seize hold of him and stamp her mark on him.

Because it told her that he wanted to mate with her.

"That's the theory," she whispered, edging closer to his lips.

"Suppose that's one way of winning this bet." He tugged her to him and claimed her mouth and her response came out as a groan as he kissed her. It was fierce, demanding, intoxicating, had her pressing against him as it lit her blood on fire, shamelessly rubbing her body against his despite the fact anyone could see them. Rune growled as he pressed his forehead to hers. "I want to win it fair and square first though."

She nodded eagerly, gasped as he gripped her hips and lifted her.

She looped her legs around his waist, wanted to tell him to be careful and not hurt himself, but he seized her mouth in another bruising kiss. She was breathless when he drew back this time and shivered as his gaze seared her.

"Might have to make it best out of three… with my injuries and all. Like a handicap." He kissed her again, his hands shifting to her backside to press her against him.

Callie moaned against his lips, on fire for him, her mind filling with wicked things she wanted to do to him.

"A handicap sounds fair," she murmured between kisses, tried not to rub against him too much as he carried her towards the cabin, stoking the fire in her blood to an inferno.

That damned little voice at the back of her mind told her not to get caught up in things, that she had more to tell him and it was only fair she told him before they were intimate again.

She grimaced, not wanting to listen to it because she feared it would spoil the moment, but she didn't want to hide things from Rune, especially something this big. She didn't want him finding out and being angry with her for not telling him.

"Wait." She cursed herself as she pressed her hands to his shoulders and stopped him from kissing her.

He tried to kiss her again.

"Wait." She pushed him back and locked her elbows this time, so he couldn't tug her to him and make her forget telling him the other half of the reason they both might pass out.

"Why? Is this because of my injuries?" he growled those words, looking as if he was going to lay down the law with her because he thought she doubted he could handle making love to her while he was healing.

She shook her head and tried to think of a delicate way to put it.

Blurted, "We should use protection."

"Protection?" He frowned and eased back, giving up trying to kiss her. He searched her eyes instead and she squirmed.

"The passing out thing… It happens between fated mates… when a female is… you know." Could she sound any lamer? She blushed, her cheeks burning with it as he just stared at her. He was going to make her spell it out for him. She couldn't bring herself to look him in the eye as she said, "I'm receptive to a male. If we don't use protection, I might get pregnant. I mean, it's rare for a female wolf to get pregnant, like with any other shifter, but I thought you should know… and just to be safe we should—"

He cut her off with a kiss, claimed her lips in a searing one that curled her toes. She sank into it again, lost herself as heat rolled through her, forgot what they had been talking about for a blissful few seconds before he moved with her and it hit her again.

She pushed against his shoulders, breaking away from his lips, and breathed, "What are you doing?"

"Making love to you," he growled and she glanced into his eyes, saw in them that he was serious as he added, "Whatever happens, I'm on board with it, Callie. I never thought I'd say this, but… I like the idea of a little cub of my own… with you."

Gods. She melted at that, at the thought of Rune taking care of their cub, raising it with the same tender care as he had Misty and Brook.

She captured his lips this time, kissed him so hard even she saw stars.

Rune kicked the door closed behind them, sending a shiver rolling down her spine, and settled her on the kitchen counter. He tore at her clothes as she fumbled with his jeans, desperate to get him naked, wild with need of him. He pulled her boots and leggings off and she moaned as he pushed her thighs apart, as he dragged her to the edge of the counter and seated himself inside her in one thrust.

Callie clung to him, fisting his top as he pumped her with long, fierce strokes, as pleasure built inside her, swift to reach a crescendo. She cried into his mouth as her body kicked and pulsed, fought the encroaching wave of darkness as it tried to roll over her. Rune grunted and his grip on her slackened for a moment as he plunged as deep as she could take him and throbbed inside her, holding her on him in the most delicious way.

He shook his head as he pitched towards her, a groggy look on his face as he slurred, "That doesn't count."

Callie cupped his nape and pulled him to her, kissed him slowly, bringing him down and building him up again at the same time. The fire he had quenched was swift to ignite again, and she wasn't sure it would ever be sated, not as long as she lived. She would always be on fire for this male.

For her bear.

He scowled at her when she broke the kiss.

"I think it should probably count. That's one out of three…" She flexed around him, ripping a grunt from him, and smiled. "But I'm a nice wolf. I'll give you a sporting chance."

"Will you now?" he positively growled those words, the heat in his gaze telling her that he liked the sound of that and knew what she was going to propose.

She pulled him to her, skated her hands over his chest and felt his heart drumming against them.

"Best out of five?" Her smile grew wicked at just the thought.

Rune growled and grabbed her. He twisted with her and carried her towards the rug in front of the fireplace. "If it's going to be five, then you're going to have to give me a better sporting chance and let me lie down. I'm injured after all. On my deathbed."

He was being overdramatic, but she didn't protest when he sat on the fur rug and laid back, holding her on top of him. She wriggled her hips, ripped a gasp from his lips that she loved as she gazed down at him. Just the thought of spending the night making love to him like this had her aching for him again, roused that primal part of her that wanted to dominate him.

They weren't going to be walking back to Black Ridge tomorrow, that was for sure.

But maybe the day after.

Once this fever had broken.

And they could both walk again.

She stared into his eyes, trying to see in them if he really wanted to mate with her, if he was contemplating crazy things like she was. She had never been one to rush into something, but this thing she had with Rune felt right. He felt right. She wanted to be with him and if he asked it of her, she would consent to being his mate right this moment, without hesitation.

"What are you thinking in there?" he husked, his voice scraping low, drowsy with passion.

"About my new pack."

He frowned at her.

Callie rotated her hips again, chasing it away. "Hoping this time it's a permanent move."

Rune relaxed again as he scowled at her. She knew it was bad of her to tease him by making it sound as if she meant to stay here, as if she was thinking about this pack and not her newest one at Black Ridge, but she was still a little scared.

Still a little afraid to take the leap.

He slid his hands up her thighs, looked close to teasing her for a moment, but then he sighed and his look turned serious. "I'm not one to live in the past, Callie. At least I try not to. I want to live in the now and look to the future, and that future is one I want with you."

Gods, this male knew how to make a female melt when he wasn't overthinking it.

She could get used to this sweet-talking side of him, one he only seemed to show to her.

She leaned over him and kissed him, savoured the way he wrapped his arms around her and returned the kiss, every gentle sweep of his lips over hers speaking to her, telling her all the things he couldn't find the courage to voice. She kissed him softly too, hoping he could hear the things she was too afraid to say, hoping he knew how much she needed him and how full her heart felt.

How she felt as if she had finally found her true home.

In his arms.

She had thought fate was cruel, had only dark times in mind for her, but it had brought her to her fated one, to her bear, and to a future she wanted with all her heart.

One that looked bright and beautiful, filled with love and happiness.

"You want to see if you can win this bet?" she murmured against Rune's lips, aching for him again.

"I'm raising the stakes." He stroked his fingers down her spine, sending a tingle along it.

Callie drew back and looked at him, a frown creasing her brow. "What are you playing for now?"

His pale blue eyes held hers, overflowing with warmth, with affection that made her breath hitch. "Your heart."

She sighed, heated from head to toe by the earnest look in his eyes, by how deeply he wanted that. "I'm afraid I can't bet that."

The warmth in his eyes faltered, his fingers tightening against her back, and she sensed the spike in his feelings, saw the dark path his thoughts were taking.

"My heart isn't mine to give." She pursed her lips, weathered his low growl as it sent another thrill chasing through her, and told herself she really had to stop teasing him, even though it was fun and revealed how badly he wanted her, how crazy he already was about her.

As crazy as she was about him.

Callie lowered her mouth towards his again, feeling sure now, certain of something and no longer afraid. She would take the leap, Rune would catch her, and together they would seize that future they both wanted.

She breathed against his lips.

"You already won it."

And claimed his with a kiss.

The End

ABOUT THE AUTHOR

Felicity Heaton is a New York Times and USA Today best-selling author who writes passionate paranormal romance books. In her books she creates detailed worlds, twisting plots, mind-blowing action, intense emotion and heart-stopping romances with leading men that vary from dark deadly vampires to sexy shape-shifters and wicked werewolves, to sinful angels and hot demons!

If you're a fan of paranormal romance authors Lara Adrian, J R Ward, Sherrilyn Kenyon, Kresley Cole, Gena Showalter, Larissa Ione and Christine Feehan then you will enjoy her books too.

If you love your angels a little dark and wicked, her best-selling Her Angel romance series is for you. If you like strong, powerful, and dark vampires then try the Vampires Realm romance series or any of her stand alone vampire romance books. If you're looking for vampire romances that are sinful, passionate and erotic then try her London Vampires romance series. Or if you like hot-blooded alpha heroes who will let nothing stand in the way of them claiming their destined woman then try her Eternal Mates series. It's packed with sexy heroes in a world populated by elves, vampires, fae, demons, shifters, and more. If sexy Greek gods with incredible powers battling to save our world and their home in the Underworld are more your thing, then be sure to step into the world of Guardians of Hades.

If you have enjoyed this story, please take a moment to contact the author at **author@felicityheaton.com** or to post a review of the book online

Connect with Felicity:
Website – http://www.felicityheaton.com
Blog – http://www.felicityheaton.com/blog/
Twitter – http://twitter.com/felicityheaton
Facebook – http://www.facebook.com/felicityheaton
Goodreads – http://www.goodreads.com/felicityheaton
Mailing List – http://www.felicityheaton.com/newsletter.php

FIND OUT MORE ABOUT HER BOOKS AT:
http://www.felicityheaton.com

Printed in Great Britain
by Amazon